Arcanum Fabulas

Tales Both Strange & Absurd,

By Bam Barrow

URBAN PIGS PRESS

© 2023 Bam Barrow

Urban Pigs Press 2023© ™®

All Rights Reserved. The moral rights of the author have been declared by the author as the owner of this work. Any reproduction in whole or part must be approved by the rights holder. This is a work of fiction. Unless otherwise indicated, all the names, characters, businesses, places, events and incidents in this book are either the product of the author's imagination or used in a fictitious manner.

Dedicated to Jay-Bird & Jenks,

for all the unending support & motivation.

Contents

A Most Wretched Reflection

Y Dwfn Dwyn

The Murder Of Debbie Cheshire

Mister Childress

Decadent Heaven

With The Grain

The Eucharist of Mara

A peculiar thing

Cult Of The White Feathers

Crawling Terror

Sunday, November 24th, 1963.

Call Me Grishka

Synesthetic Therapy: Decadent Meditation For The Middle Class Eccentric.

A Most Wretched Reflection

I don't know how to describe to you how I feel. I cry, yet I have no tears. Hell, I have no cheeks with which to catch them, nor do I have the eyes to secrete them - not in the way that you're familiar with anyway. I scream daily at the pain, but there is no sound, for there is no mouth. I guess it could be compared to that nasty feeling you hold in the pit of your stomach. That rancid ball of grief that just will not go away. What kind of mockery is this? What madness? Why am I still here?!

I remember what happened before all this. Oh the pain. Oh god the unbearable agony. The weeks in hospital. The negative bloods. The first time I vomited blood. The last time I saw her face. Oh how I *wish* it was the last time I'd seen that face.

I discovered the truth about *him* almost immediately after. There was no transition. He moved into my house, slept in my bed, ate my food and had my wife before my flesh had even made it into the crematorium. Ah, the crematorium. Very clever. No autopsy on religious grounds, no excavation at a later date. I can't knock the fool-proof plan.

She told my mother that she spread my ashes in Wevolow, where we first met. A lie. She gave them to *him* and he dumped them out into a street bin around the corner from the morgue.

Three years before my death they had been at it behind my back. Three long years. The Cutting Duke showed me all of it. All the covert liaisons, all the places in the house they played grotesque fetish sex games while I was away on business. The place where he first strangled her unconscious and had his way with her body. The place at the back of the pantry where they hid the antimony. In the little hole where the mice used to hide.

The Alabaster Duke showed me eating the food and drink laced with antimony during those last few months, not a care in the world, still calling *him* my best friend, still head over heels for *her*. I got very sick. Very, very sick. About as sick as you can be. Have you ever watched yourself deteriorate slowly in the third person? No, I guess not. How about watching yourself desperately accepting care from the people who did this to you, only to watch them leave the room to fuck each other and snigger at their diabolical plan? It hurts worse than the months I clung to life for her. It hurts worse than my organs shutting down. It hurts worse than that fucking look on her face as I lost consciousness for the very last time.

  I want revenge. I beg for it, and I know he has the power to grant me it if he wanted to, but he's having far too much fun with my own personal misery. I suppose I asked for it. That taciturn megalomaniac in the ward. Who *was* he? Why did he have to show me that book?! Why did I *read* it?! Why did I forsake my god for this abominable situation? Is this my punishment for forsaking my god, or is it part of the Codex Cthxs' will? I got no answer from him. He does not speak. I don't know if he can, with his solid pearlescent face. He shows rather than tells. I'm not sure if this creature is wholeheartedly evil though. I don't think it understands what evil is. It is a presence that feels beyond the pettiness of human morality. Something more. Something incomprehensible. It doesn't seem to hate, love or care at all.

Well, the days whittled on, and on the first month anniversary of my passing, they held an orgy in my study. Eight men and three women and... well, I'd rather not talk about it. I still don't understand why she never was in the least bit adventurous with me, I would have leapt at the chance to have a story or two to tell. I always thought she, out of the two of us, was the traditionalist. I would've done anything for her. I DID do everything for her. Wretched little bitch.

Of course, she got the house. £1.2 million in assets in total and £257,000 in insurance payouts. I watched them sell my stuff, the things I held most dear, and spend it all on a lavish trip to the Caribbean together, a small yacht docked in Wevolow, and boarding school for the son we had together. I have no idea what happened with my son, my gaze does not ever leave her, and she never saw or spoke of him again. Perhaps that's best. I have little hope left in my soul, I'm not sure I could bear it if I knew.

I watched them have two children together, I watched him leave. I watched him come back with diseases and I watched her hit him. I watched him hit her back, and I watched their two little girls absorb all of this madness - the fights, the infidelity, the physical and sexual abuse. I won't lie, at first I felt like justice was being done, but after years of watching little Sadie and Zoe suffer, I became numb to it. By now I had long come to terms with who she really was. I wanted out, but I'd begged the book to be with her forever. What a fool.

She got old fast. Her forties and fifties were not kind, and her face began to reflect her own misdeeds. When she was forty-one, the teenage girls left for good. There were no repercussions for either of their behaviours. When she was fifty-eight, he died in a drunken car wreck. She rarely left the house after that. Just sat there reading and crying and wandering about the house. She was weak and broken. And that's how I found a way in.

It felt great, the first time I scared her, I don't really know how I did it. It's hard to explain to someone with a body how you could possibly knock a picture of your nemesis off the wall without having the fingers to touch it. But I did. Soon I was terrorising her at every opportunity I could - I'd pinch her body while she slept. Move objects around when she wasn't looking. She'd lived an entire life since me, so naturally she assumed it was him taunting her from beyond the grave. No. He didn't read that book, did he - I did. The one you poisoned to death. Do you remember? Do you even care? Of course not.

I was having so much fun with it. Revenge! Finally! Nothing despicable, but fun for me, nonetheless. But like everything, the fun didn't last. I think the Duke got sick of my shenanigans to be honest. So he allowed me one last fright. One evening, she was busy brushing her teeth in the bathroom. I was just watching, as I am cursed to do, when I noticed with a start, that I could see myself in the mirror. This, I had not been able to do in over fifty years. I looked horrid. What a monstrous disaster! What a wretched fiend I had become. This is too much! What a grizzly misery I am! I cannot possibly let her see this decrepit monstrosity, this sorry form of existence! I tried to move, but I am not permitted to move away from her. Not ever. She spat into the sink and looked back up to check her face. We immediately made eye contact. Eye contact for the first time in fifty years, and for the very last time before she dropped dead then and there like a stone.

I watched the maggots eat her. I watched her fluids sink into the wooden floor of the bathroom, staining it with her shape and I watched them scrape her remains up from the boards when they found her months later. She went right through the floor into the study. Now I'm stuck in this room where she died from the shock of my grizzled form. People sometimes come to look into the mirror, some say they see me, some don't. It makes no difference, I am here for eternity. I am to be with her forever. The bits of her stuck in this house between the bathroom and the study, in the gap under the floorboards where the mice used to hide.

Y Dwfn Dwyn

Malachite. The saviour of the bronze age. With it, we ascended from the stone and the bone to the ways of the blade and the axe. We stole it from the mountain's face, plucking away at the limestone surfaces with little more than rocks and pieces of skeleton. The curious material was soft and we ground it down to a fine pastel-green powder, and we put it to the fire, and pulled out of the ashes a metal that would give us wealth, status and power above all others who did not know its secrets.

But what we have is never enough.

We dug. Endlessly, we dug. We chipped away at more and more precious malachite ore until there was none left on the surface to take. We could not break the limestone with sticks and stones alone, but we soon became desperate enough to slowly pluck out the mountain's veins.

And so we went down, down under the mountain, digging out the ore veins until great caverns and tunnels opened up to us and showed us the way to even greater spoils. Generation after generation we chipped away at the treasure beneath the mountain. When the tunnels closed in tight we sent our children down into the long dark, for greed knows neither age nor creed, and we dominated the land with our hard-won finery.

Day One

Why anyone would want to come all the way up here for pleasure, I have no idea. It is so cold. Stinging, biting cold. The elements are so harsh that I find it hard to believe they don't have a malicious will of their own. It feels angry up here, and wild. It feels similar to being trapped inside the oppressive inescapable heat of a city summer, where the endless concrete absorbs all the heat of the day and the hot air lies stagnant between the mammoth buildings. Yesterday I had my feet up watching trash TV in the warm comfort of my heated Brixton flat and today I'm up in North Wales in the height of autumn, looking for my shithead brother, freezing my bollocks off in a place that should be left well enough alone. What good am I in a place like this? I nearly had a cardiac trotting up Stanmore Hill for fuck's sake. But Ma insisted on it, and so off into the wild I went on this wild goose chase. I didn't have much choice in the end. I owe her a lot of scratch, and she uses that against me.

I slept almost all the way from Corley services near Birmingham to Pen-y-Pass and had the fright of my life when Drake, who was Richard's best friend, slapped me awake. He didn't want me to miss the gargantuan growths of rock dwarfing us from either side of the road. I felt so small. I realised immediately that the intimidating masses of the mountains scared me. Drake was in awe, as if it wasn't the hundredth time he'd seen these very hills. I have never seen anything like it, and I hope to god I never see anything like it again.

Another hour or so went by in relative silence until we finally lost the low sun behind a huge swathe of tall outcrops. We sailed down a hill, creeping under shadow towards the ominous black doom that dominated the horizon. We pulled into a cut in the road next to a Jeep Wrangler and Drake sprung from the car like a gazelle, taking in lungfuls of fresh mountain air. I crawled out from the comfort of the heated seats and pulled up my hood and zipped up my coat, which did nothing to hamper the probing cold.

"This is it," he said. It definitely felt like 'it' to me. I couldn't help but loosen the despair in my heart.

"There's just no way," I said.

"Don't lose hope," replied Drake.

I sat on the bonnet of the car, staring up at what was to be our mammoth task as Drake unloaded and fiddled with equipment. My eyes were fixed upon a little speck in the distance, slowly moving about, high upon a lofty ridge. A sheep maybe, I thought, till the thing began to slowly descend towards the cars, and I could make out the limbs of a person. I watched in awe as they elegantly danced about the rock face, finding the best route down, but never stalling. It was the body of Diana - Richard's wife, coming down, straight for us.

"Johnathan Crawley," She yelped, her voice echoing around the landscape like a war horn. "You are the last person on earth I'd expect to see all the way up here!"

I waved to her nonchalantly as she leaped across a small trickling brook and made her way down to us.

"He was blackmailed," said Drake, appearing from behind the car. The two formally embraced and Drake tossed her a bottle of water.

"I expect nothing less," she said. "But any extra pair of eyes is another chance at finding something."

"Well, let's get this over and done with," I said, already shivering.

"You go for it mate, if you've got a death wish," said Drake.

"We've already lost the light. We're done until sunrise," said Diana.

"To the hotel then," I muttered naively.

"Here's your hotel," quipped Drake, chucking a tent bag on the ground. Both of them laughed. My heart sank.

Day Two

I don't know if it was the clean air, the cosiness of the tiny tent or the utter quiet, but I slept like I hadn't in years. I woke with the sun at around 7am, finding Drake and Diana deep in conversation around a small gas stove. I wandered over to them bleary-eyed and slumped down on a foldable chair they'd set for me. Drake poured me a coffee, Diana was heating canned meatballs in a mess-tin. They invited me into the conversation.

"Before the sun went behind the cliffs last night, I found this," she said, passing me a sandwich bag with a dark object inside. A familiar shape to pretty much anybody.

"Richard's phone," I said. "Have you searched it? There may be a clue."

"It's dead. I found it in a small stream. A bloody lucky find. I've flagged the location so we can find it again. If worst comes to worst we might be able to pull the harddrive."

"Well, we have our heading for today then," said Drake. "I suggest we get going as soon as we can. No sense in wasting any time."

Three long hours we trekked up the side of that rock, likely because of my own neglected health. Rocks and moss and grass wandered by as I scrambled up with everything I had, but it seemed that any time I glanced upwards, Drake and Diane were standing still above me, waiting for me to catch up. I was doing my best but it was hard going. I was boiling under my layers and then freezing the moment I took anything off. Still, though it was my first foray into the wild, I persisted, following the other two with everything I had.

At length we came to a flat outcrop where I was allowed a short break from the back-breaking ascent. I turned to face our progress and found that we were indeed far up the mountain, our cars in the cleft below only specks of white and grey. I turned back to face the rock, feeling a little pinch of vertigo and once I caught my breath we continued, though we had now begun to cross the terrain laterally rather than climbing upwards, out of the view of the road and over the mountain's shoulder into true wilderness. The rolling hills and jagged rocks went on as far as the eye could see and I couldn't help the lump in my throat as we travelled. We are never going to find my brother. Over marshy bogs we trudged, and through thick moss beds that breathed with life under foot. The occasional mountain sheep popped up a head at us, a face of disdain for the trespassers spoiling his peace and quiet.

We located Diana's flag just after midday and just beside it a tiny stream quietly snuck through the indent it had made in the grass of the hill. Each of us set out in different directions to scour the immediate area for clues, but it was useless. We found nothing and the East wind whipped at us angrily, hampering every effort. We met back at the flag an hour later, freezing cold and wet shin-down from the boggy ground. It was hopeless. I stared up at the top of the dark monster which still loomed hundreds of feet above our heads, its intimidating mass hiding the body of my brother, mocking me for my folly. My stupidity at even trying.

Richard had never really been the same since all that business in Croxton. I always trusted my brother, but the things he had said happened there were farfetched to say the least and did significant damage to his reputation at Scotland Yard. He lost his job four years ago and replaced a lucrative career as a detective inspector, with wild hunts in the wilderness for things I can only describe as occult in nature. By the time Drake and I first touched down in Wales it had been three weeks since he'd disappeared. Search teams and rescue helicopters had found nothing, so I couldn't help but wonder what good it was for me to be there. What the fuck could I do that a team of professionals couldn't? I was almost certain he was gone and that the idea of us three fools finding him was completely daft. With this in mind and defeat in my heart, I decided to make my way back down the mountain to the camp, without the others.

Day Three

When I arrived back at our little base camp yesterday afternoon, I stripped myself of wet and soiled clobber and collapsed in a mess in my tent. A rookie mistake; it was dark when I awoke and I remained awake for the rest of the night.

The wind lashed at the flimsy fabric of my tent. The rain joined it at 2am. By three, I was hallucinating terrible sounds hiding in the cacophony of noise. There were voices, malicious and angry, screaming down on us, though I couldn't make out the words. Claws scratched at the fabric walls, sending the entire tent quivering. The static storm thundered through my brain like a freight train until I couldn't take it anymore. I had to go. Had to leave this place, take Drake's car and make for the nearest town. He could hitch a ride with Diane and we could all meet up once they'd given up searching. I pulled on all the clothes I had inside the tent and braced myself for a drenching. I ripped up the zip and lunged upwards, fleeing from the open mouth of my torture chamber and out of this hellhole.

I was blinded. The horrid voices rang out and faded in my head, but I wasn't being drenched by any rain. Overwhelmed with what was going on, I closed my eyes and slumped to my knees on the ground. It was morning, and the rain had stopped hours ago. I burst into tears.

Drake drove me to town that morning and I checked into a hotel. I don't know if he was angry at me, sympathetic or just upset at the whole situation. The whole drive down was silent. So that's how it was. Abandoned to lick my own selfish wounds in Llandudno. The town was beautiful, not that I saw much of it. I ventured out just for food and spent the rest of the time in my room puzzled by the month's events.

Day Five

I thought Drake would never show back up, and I'd arranged to get the train back to London the morning he hammered on my door at 3am. The moment I turned the handle he barged in, sopping wet and white as a sheet. He crossed my room and flicked on the kettle, preparing two coffees by tipping grounds into cups straight out of the can. I fetched him towels, and he slunk down on my chair shaking like a shitting dog.

"She's gone mate, she's gone," he said. "Oh god it was horrible."

I tried to ask him what was going on, but he wasn't making much sense at all.

"Followed it up, up into the rock. Miles and miles of it. Slimy, pink death. They know. They know."

"What do they know?"

"They know your mind. The colours of the sources. Every leaf on every tree. A network. They see us all."

I helped Drake get undressed, noticing a considerable patch of dried blood inside his left ear. I pushed him into a hot shower and tipped out the muddy coffees he'd made and poured us fresh cups of tea. He reappeared forty-five minutes later, calmer, if not still shaken to the core. I didn't attempt to speak with him, I just handed him a robe and the mug of tea and let him breathe. After some agonising minutes he began to spill.

"We… We found him, John. We found him. Looked about for two days, didn't find a shred. At a loss, didn't know what to do. Yesterday we set off at first light. We followed the stream. We went up into the hills, up for hours. Found the source, coming from inside the mountain, a little gap blocked with rubble. We sat there, ready to give up. Then we heard it. Tap…Tap… Tap… coming from the mountain wall. Crouched low to the small hole the stream was leaking from. Tap… Tap… Tap… Metal on stone. I yelled into the hole. Tapping stopped, but no response. Then there it was again -

tap, tap. We started to remove the rubble. Took us hours. Behind it all was a tunnel. We went in, followed the sounds. Never seen so many tunnels. Some went up, some down, some snaked off in all different directions. We followed the sounds, followed the stream water, deeper and deeper into the mountain. I don't know how long for, but when I got back out again it was dark. We were slowly descending, but the water was still flowing back and up from where we came. I don't know how. We came to a cavern under the ground as wide as it was tall, must've been the size of a football field. Horrid slime all over the walls. Smelt like rot and sea water. Water was coming up from a hole in the centre of the cave, crawling up the walls and out through different tunnels. The slime was writhing. At the back of the space we found him. His body was alive, but he wasn't in it. It was something else. Something hollow and dark. He stood there, arms outstretched, staring at us with bulbous eyes but no real expression, no reaction to us whatsoever besides those eyes which followed us. We called out to him. Tried to speak to him. He just watched with those big bug eyes. I put my hand on his shoulder and it felt like stone. Tried to grab him by the wrist but it wouldn't budge no matter how hard I pulled. Diana was beside herself. Hugging him, crying, we were both crying. Trying to pry him from his position, but he wouldn't move, or couldn't move. Just kept watching us with those unblinking eyes. The slime was coming down the walls, some of it was changing colour from a rancid, dark moss to a pigskin pink, covered in little teeth. I started to back away in fear, but Diana couldn't let Richard go. Some of the slime rolled away from the walls of the cave, taking a horrible shape like a snake but looking more like the tongue of a clam. Whatever they were, they were on Diana before I could do anything, pulling her to the ground, turning back into slime and covering her there on the ground. She was screaming and choking under it all. I tried to stop it, but those things were already coming for me. I slipped and fell. I tried to escape, but one got me on the face. I pulled it off right away, but it had already infected me with ten thousand years of hallucinations in my mind. I saw it all, John. It was mother nature in its primordial form, up there, in the heart of the mountain. I saw the day it was discovered and what it did to the children who dug it up. I saw it watching from every living thing rooted to the ground. It knows everything. Everything we've done to the planet, every sin we have committed as a species. It knows all and it IS all."

It is safe to say, although I am not proud of it, that rather than suggest we contact the authorities or go back up to the mountain together to do something, Drake and I fled North Wales that night and were back in London by noon. Drake has never really been the same. He stays inside as much as he can and has a fit any time he is near any kind of park or garden. I don't know what came of Diana, we have both avoided the situation for many years. I can only assume that she is also filed as missing, presumed dead. Who knows. Neither of us want to leave our concrete havens. Sometimes, when the wind is right and you pass a particularly malicious tree, you can hear their voices wailing in the wind and any time that happens, I just head back inside for as long as I can.

The Murder Of Debbie Cheshire

Fresh developments are coming in tonight as the ex-boyfriend of slain university student Debbie Cheshire was arrested earlier this morning on suspicion of murder. Mr Jared Shaye, aged thirty-one, was arrested without incident in Bristol by detectives at the home of a friend. Mr Shaye fled the county shortly after the heinous attack three months ago, which left Miss Cheshire, 20, fighting for her life. She subsequently succumbed to her injuries after thirty-nine hours in intensive care. Mr Shaye is being held in Bristol and is expected to be transferred back to Ipswich to appear in court for an arraignment hearing on Monday.

Miss Cheshire was discovered in the early hours of the sixteenth of February on the street outside of her address in Primrose Hill, Ipswich, by a dog walker. The victim had been stabbed multiple times and appeared delirious from severe blood loss. Emergency services were called and she succumbed to her injuries two days later. Mr Shaye, a person of interest from the early stages of the investigation, was nowhere to be found.

Shaye and Miss Cheshire had allegedly broken up four days previous to the attack. Friends and family of the victim have stated that the relationship between the two seemed to be stable and loving on the outside, but in the last few weeks that Jared had become increasingly obsessive and aggressive towards Debbie, especially during times that they would spend apart from each other. What appeared to be a happy relationship on the surface had started to become increasingly abusive, though it wasn't until police detective examiners analysed Miss Cheshire's mobile phone that the case was turned on its head.

Deleted writer notes recovered from the phone, detailing intimate details of the couple's life together helped to paint a picture for police as to just how a one-night stand could possibly end up in a grizzly murder.

Now of course there is a lot of information concerning the contents of Debbie Cheshire's phone that is not yet public knowledge, but the little that we do know tells a story of lies, deceit and manipulation from the very beginning and it is presumed that arguments from both sides will be presented to the judge as to whether this legally circumstantial evidence will be allowed to be presented in court when the time comes.

The couple met in the summer of last year at Burrs, a Colchester nightclub infamous for its wild and often out of control parties. The two, according to Miss Cheshire's writing, met and danced and after spending some hours together at the club, they hailed a taxi and went back to Shaye's flat to hook up.

It was love at first sight for the Essex University student, although she lamented in her notes that the feeling did not appear to be mutual. Shaye ghosted Cheshire's calls and messages for almost a fortnight until a chance meeting came upon the two again at the very same club. Cheshire then managed to seduce Shaye and again, they left the club to get together.

That second night they spent together was where Debbie Cheshire first implemented her grand plan to win over Jared. She allegedly waited for Mr Shaye to fall asleep beside her and when he did, she stuck a high-strength nicotine patch to his back. Shaye, who was not a smoker, absorbed enough nicotine that night for someone with a twenty-a-day habit. The patch was removed before the man woke up, and the two parted ways a second time, but this time, it was Shaye who pursued Cheshire the next day.

The plan had taken effect, and every time the two met up, Cheshire would spike Shaye's system with nicotine. With what some have described as her modern-day love potion, she would then leave, causing Mr Shaye to go into severe nicotine withdrawal. The subtleties of the devious trick led Jared to believe subconsciously that he needed Debbie, feeling a sense of relaxation when she was there, and suffering extreme agitation and insomnia when she wasn't. He had become chemically dependent on her, a feeling he mistook for infatuation.

Miss Cheshire's plan, it seemed, had worked. She had the man she wanted at her every beck and call. But as the besotted behaviour ran into obsession, it was clear that the young woman's scheme to ensnare the unaware Shaye had backfired. Phone records between the two show an incessant barrage of calls and text messages sent from Shaye to Cheshire during any occasion that the two were apart. What began a fairly innocent, if deceptive relationship, soon began to become overwhelming for the girl. Unable to study, work or socialise without her boyfriend there, it is safe to say that things were getting a little too much.

As previously stated, weeks before the murder occured, the state of the relationship had degraded significantly. While Cheshire continued to drug Shaye, it is apparent in her conversations with friends and in her own writings that she was struggling to cope with Shaye's overbearing behaviour. It is believed that the following breakup and severe nicotine withdrawal served as a factor in the man's vicious attack, but we will not be able to understand Jared Shaye's side of the story, unless he chooses to speak to authorities.

There stands a large question that, going forward, will be the subject of much debate over the next few months regarding the case. While the act of murder will always be inexcusable, abhorrent and unforgivable, one can't quite help but wonder if the blame lies solely on the perpetrator in this case. Miss Cheshire obviously can't speak for herself beyond the evidence she has left behind, but it will be interesting to see just how this case unfolds in the near future.

Mister Childress

Joyce peeked through the net curtain once again, peering down the dark length of Platt street - the fourth time she'd done so in just as many minutes. She'd tried tea, she'd tried nicotine, but these failed to soften her anxiety. One could almost say that they made things worse. She flicked the curtain back into place and threw herself onto the sofa for the umpteenth time. The television was on, but she could not process the conversations filling the room, for the adrenaline was all-consuming. She heard laughter. She never heard the joke. Maybe the world was just laughing at *her*. She touched the screen of her phone once again, lighting her face with a fluorescent pallor. No reply. *I'll unlock it*, she thought, although there was still nothing to see when she did so.

She got up again and resumed her pacing of the room, thumbing her phone, rolling it over and over in her hand. *Maybe I missed a notification,* she thought, but when she opened her daughter's text chain, the last message remained. It was from herself, and it said -

Okay, please be careful. I'll see you when you get home.

Twenty minutes had gone by now.

Twenty minutes! She should be home by now, I should call her. No. NO. You promised.

Another peek down the street. Nobody there.

I'm going to call her.

Joyce opened her phone's call log, her thumb hovering over her daughter's name. She hesitated. She promised Shelly she wouldn't pester her. Below her daughter's name was the name of Joyce's best friend, Laurie, who lived down the street - their daughters were best friends too. To stop herself from breaking the promise she'd made, she forced her thumb downwards and pressed Laurie's name instead. Laurie answered the call in fewer than three rings.

"Joyce, sweetie, everything okay?"

"Did Hannah come home yet?"

"No, not yet, she texted me about 20 minutes ago, did Shelly not message you?"

"Yes, she did."

"Well then, they're on their way, they'll be back any minute."

"Oh Laurie, I cannot bear this transition," Joyce burst down the phone.

"I know, I'm nervous too, but our babies are growing up now, it's time they earned some independence."

"Oh god! What if they're trying to call right now? They won't be able to reach either of us!?"

"Joyce, honey, you need to relax. Do your breathing. Do you want me to pop over for a cuppa?"

"No… no it's ok, I've just got to get a hold of myself. I've worked myself up too much again! Maybe I'll go and wait for her from the garden."

"Joyce, you promised her."

"Yes, yes I did. Oh god. Okay."

"Hold on," said Laurie, background noise filling the phone line. "Yes! Joyce, Hannah just walked through the door."

"Oh thank god."

Try as she might, Joyce could no longer resist temptation, finding herself waiting at the front door for her beloved daughter. She decided to smoke a cigarette out there, that being a convenient reason to be outside.

Across the street, another neighbour stirred. Winston Childress was his name, a recent addition to Platt Street, relative to the other lifers who dwelt there anyway. He emerged from his front door and likewise sat on the porch, puffing away on an old pipe.

Catching his gaze from across the road, Joyce found herself realising that she knew very little about Mr Childress at all. Ignoring her own blind ignorance and relying solely on judgement, she began to ponder the peculiarities of the man across the road, who she'd never properly or openly spoken to except for that one particular time she couldn't bear to think about.

He never closed his drapes, always wore dark sunglasses no matter the time of day and kept his front lawn empty and unadorned. He carried with him a fancy walking stick, but had no limp, not to mention the fact that he had been seen out in the daytime without it. He was caught on many occasions, by neighbours around them, spying up and down the street from the circular attic window at the top of the house. The police had been called and had come out to speak to him, but they informed the concerned complainants that he was 'well within his rights to look out of his windows.'

Perhaps it was the secret that the two strangers had between them that sourced her paranoia. Shelly could never find out that the one-time day-drunk flit the two had had five and a half years ago was the real reason her dad had left them. Hell, they hadn't even stopped amidst the fury to learn each other's names at the time. It was a foolish mistake and one Joyce still felt the sting of. She hadn't touched a drink since. In her mind, the blame lay solely at the feet of Winston for seducing her and the bottle of rum that had enslaved her to a life of housewive's misery, and the secret that lived inside of her like a tumour consumed her.

Mr Childress was the first to break his gaze. He turned his head to the left and with a plume of smoke, set his gaze down the road, towards Joyce's daughter. Shelly was there, two houses away, and across the street from her walked a boy of a similar age in the same direction. Joyce's fears were over then, and she accepted her daughter into her arms in a loving embrace, feeling the November chill upon her coat. She let Shelly past as she stamped out her cigarette, noticing the boy enter the Childress home, Mr Childress still staring through his sunglasses at her from the porch.

"Joyce." He nodded.

"Stan." She replied.

She shuddered, and went inside, letting the cat stroll in, in front of her.

"How did it go sweetheart?" Joyce asked enthusiastically.

"It was great!" Proclaimed Shelly, quickly stripping her autumn attire. "It's hot in here!"

"Nice and toasty. The walk back was okay? No issues?"

"No, no it was fine. I was with Hannah the whole time and Jam followed us home didn't you boy! We watched his eyes shining all the way down the street through the gardens."

The black cat was purring heavily, rubbing himself against Shelly's legs. She knelt down to give him a fuss.

"Aww, you've got a little protector there! That makes me feel a little better."

"You okay mum?" Shelly asked, taking the cue.

"Yes darling, I'm fine. I was a little worried, but I am your mum, I have to be!"

Dinner was quiet for the two of them. Joyce was still ruminating over the enigmatic and eccentric Mr Childress. Nobody knew what the man did for a living, he never seemed to be away from his house more than a couple of hours at a time for groceries and such. Equally as perplexing was the fact that the Childress mother was a missing part of the picture. Joyce thought to herself at that moment, that she had never actually taken the time to ask Winston any of these unanswered questions herself, but now, through her shame, she'd left the mysteries live on for far too long, leaving a faux pas of nosiness in her mind. It wouldn't be right if she were to suddenly start poking around now. The last thing she wanted was to open wounds that she had so far successfully avoided. Bury it down, Joyce. Bury it deep.

"Do you ever talk to the sickly Childress boy?" She asked, quite out of nowhere.

"His name is Jacob, Mum."

"Jacob! Yes! He goes to your club?"

"Yeah he goes. We've played a few games together, he's very good, but not very chatty."

"Strange family."

"Oh he's fine, just quiet. He and Hannah seem to like each other. I asked her if there was something going on between them, but she shushed me and went all red!"

"Oh, good!" Joyce exclaimed a little too enthusiastically.

"What?"

"Oh, nothing darling."

The after-school chess club ran every Tuesday and Thursday night, and like clockwork, the girls stayed behind and the mothers worried about them walking home in the dark. It wasn't unfounded, all this anxiety over their children. It wouldn't be the first time a child went missing in the town of Durston, Suffolk. In fact if something were to happen to one of them, they'd be the sixth in three decades. The present list of five had vanished into thin air and no sign of them had ever been found. Some say they wandered off into the vast forest bordering the town, some think it to be the work of a predator hiding among them. Nobody really knew for certain and although the timespan of the cases was vast, it didn't stop a paranoid black cloud from looming over every parent in the town, especially when the long nights drew in. But the children continued to grow, and the parents only worried more as they were forced to begrudgingly loosen the leash.

***

"Are you sure you want to go tonight?" Asked Joyce, in mid-December, her worry betraying her. "You know Hannah won't be there don't you, she's got her uncle's funeral this afternoon."

"I know, I'll be fine, she's coming round after I get home."

"I could come and pick you up if you'd like? It's no bother."

"Mum, for god's sake!" Shelly snapped. "I'll be fine!"

"...As long as you're sure, sweetie. I just worry."

Neither Hannah nor Jacob were at school that day. The day went by slowly without her friend, but Shelly stuck it out on her own. She found it extremely strange too that she hadn't received any messages all day. She thought that maybe she'd pushed a little too hard with her mum, snapping like she did, but it had to be said. It was too much stress to bear and Shelly was a responsible girl, her mother knew that.

Chess club went by, she won three games, lost one. Finally, she was ready to head home. She looked at her phone before leaving the school's main building... still no messages from Hannah or her mother. She'd better get home quick and patch things up. As promised though, she sent her mum the text she sent every Tuesday and Thursday:

All finished, now leaving, see you in a bit.

The frigid air assaulted her face as she pushed through the school's main entrance. She pulled up the zip of her coat as far as it would go and made off into the cold night air.

She did admit to herself that the shadows had an extra air of foreboding without her usual company, which she quickly put down to the jitters of being alone in the dark. She marched ahead, far swifter than usual, trying to ignore the chill air and the heebie jeebies trying to swallow her. Finally she reached the top of Platt Street. All was quiet. Everything seemed right enough.

About four houses into her trek, she noticed a dark puddle by the road on the opposite side. It hadn't rained that day, so the deep shadow perplexed her. She stomped along, keeping her eyes affixed, trying to figure out what exactly the thing was. It wasn't long until it became all too apparent. Lying in the road by the opposite footpath was the body of a large black cat.

Panic took her. She recognised the shape now. The legs, the tail. That was Jam lying in the road. She flew across the road towards the cat and knelt down beside him, tears welling up in her eyes. She laid a hand on his furry body - still warm, still breathing. She gently pushed her hands underneath him to pick him up, and that's when the trap was sprung, for she was too occupied to notice Winston Childress sneaking up on her from behind.

From the shadows he came, like a storm, swift and terrible, a pillowcase in one hand, the handle of his cane in the other, which now protruded forth a nine-inch sticking blade. He descended upon Shelly before she even noticed he was there and threw the pillowcase over her head, the cold blade resting at her throat. He pulled her to her feet by the armpits and growled like the predator she now knew he was.

"March."

With his arms wrapped around her and a blade to her throat, she had no choice but to obey her captor and march to her doom towards the Childress house.

She stumbled up the porch steps, he pushed her through the door. She fell with a whimper.

"Stay down." Barked Winston. "I'm sorry it had to be like this."

He pulled the pillowcase from her head and held the blade pointed at her torso.

"Don't move."

She was petrified. Her mum was right all along. She felt in that moment an unbearable pit of agony as she felt all the emotions her mother would have to go through once she realised her daughter was gone. That same tearful hopelessness she'd seen from residents before. The same ghosts in the eyes of the parents she knew had lost their children to this monster who lived across the street. She was sobbing and she didn't even realise it. She was begging, pleading for her life for the sake of her poor mum.

"Look, just lay there, I know it's bad. Just stay. Stay there." The Durston murderer said, quite empathetically, which caught Shelly off guard. She did as she was told out of shock more than anything.

An age went by as she lay there, the blade so close to puncturing any one of her vital organs. How long had passed? Seconds? Minutes? She couldn't tell. At some point in her capture in the hallway of the Childress household, the front door clicked open behind them. It was Jacob, the boy, carefully carrying the limp body of the black cat. Shelly despaired.

"Jacob! No?! You're part of this?!"

"Of course I am," said the boy with an eerie air of calm. "Don't worry, you're safe now."

"Safe?!" Shelly cracked a smile at the sheer absurdity of the situation, "Are you out of your mind?"

Winston withdrew his sticking blade as Jacob locked the door and pocketed the keys. He returned the handle of the walking stick to its elegant shaft, placing it by the door. He then squatted down by the perplexed prisoner.

"Look, I'm sorry to do this to you, Shelly, I really am, but tonight is the night and I couldn't stand idly by." Winston spewed.

She didn't know what to say. Her beloved Jam lay there motionless beside her. Her two neighbours towered over her. Jacob broke the silence, noting the girl's gaze.

"I gave him a strong sedative wrapped in some ham. He'll be fine in a couple of hours, just a bit groggy."

"What is going on?" Shelly blurted. Winston held out a hand.

"Come with me," he said.

He led her across the hall into the Childress living room, dazed and confused. She cast her eyes around the modest lounge and saw something she did not expect.

"Mum!" She screamed and leapt over to her mother lying prone across the sofa. She wasn't right, not at all. Her glazed eyes peered at Shelly and she smiled.

"Oh my daughter. Oh you're safe at last."

"What have you done to her?!" Shelly demanded, now flooding with rage. Winston stepped forth carrying two glasses of water fetched by Jacob.

"I'm afraid Mrs Dyer was quite out of sorts today, once the situation was adequately explained. I gave her a little seroquel to calm the nerves."

"We're safe now Shelly," Joyce said softly.

"What the fuck is going on here?" Shelly demanded.

"When you're ready, go with dad," said Jacob.

"Mum, what is going on?" Shelly asked, holding her mother's hand.

"I thought I was going to lose you," she said.

"Come," said Winston. "I'll explain upstairs. Here, you can have this if you want." He gestured down to her with his ornate walking stick. She instinctively pulled the sticking blade handle from it and tentatively followed the strange man up the stairs.

Up two flights they went, ending up in the attic, where Shelly observed all kinds of military and forensic equipment. She didn't know what most of it was, exactly, but each object had militaristic or clinical characteristics enough for her to draw a sufficient conclusion. Cameras, night vision equipment, beakers with different chemicals stagnating inside. The room was strewn with notebooks, posters and sheets all hastily scribbled on in an awful doctor's style handwriting.

"What is all this?" She asked, still clutching the blade with white knuckles. Winston handed her something. It was a laminate with his picture on it, some sort of high-ranking military ID. Winston had moved over to the round window and was gazing out at the street below.

"I am a nuclear physicist by trade, Shelly, or rather I used to be. I worked heavily behind closed doors during the '03 campaign of Iraq. In '04, I had my accident. Look out there."

Winston gestured out of the little round window. Shelly joined him, looking out into the dimly lit street.

"What do you see?" Winston asked.

"Nothing," said Shelly, tiring from the riddles. "Just the street."

"Look at your house, then count three houses to the left. In the bushes. What do you see there?"

She looked. She saw nothing. There was nothing there.

"Look, what is all this abou..."

"Shush!" Snapped Winston in a harsh whisper. "Wait for the car!"

She watched as a lone car came by, headlights illuminating the street. Staring at the bushes, she thought for a split second she spied two reflective eyes staring up at them.

"There!" Exclaimed Winston. "Did you see it?"

"It's a cat mate," sighed Shelly. "We see Jam's eyes light up like that when he follows us home at night."

"See, there! That is where you are mistaken, young lady. Those ARE the eyes you have been seeing, not Jam's. I've been observing the street for weeks, your cat rarely leaves your garden at night. You've been followed home every week by *that*."

"So we've been followed home by a different cat, Stan. Who gives a shit. Are you going to explain yourself or are you gonna keep fucking with me?"

Shelly gripped the blade, raising it slightly. Winston was quite taken aback by the strong will of this girl.

"It is important that I ease you in, Shelly. I've already done enough wrong tonight, I need you to understand the reason without it being too much at once."

"So out with it then!"

"As I said, in '04, I had my accident. I won't bore you with the details but suffice to say that the accident involved radiation and my eyes have been permanently damaged for almost twenty years."

Winston removed his dark glasses, revealing a horrid pair of eyes that made Shelly gasp. They were milky, but red, an awful colour for eyes, with scar tissue lining the edges of where the white should have been.

"My god!" She squealed.

"Yes, hideous, I know. That's why I wear these. Apparently they do nothing to put people at ease! Will you put them on?"

"What?"

"Please, just put them on. Look outside, where I told you."

She did as she was asked and looked outside again, only this time it wasn't just darkness she saw. Down by her neighbour's house, four doors down behind the bushes, a shapeless mass now sat, with several spots of undulating fluorescent colours flickering and dampening. She could see the full shape of it down there, through the foliage. She removed the glasses from her face and again, there was only darkness.

"They're special glasses for my eyes," said Winston. "Polarised lenses with other filters and feats of technology. I've been watching it for years."

"It?!"

"It has made several appearances across town," he said. "I am certain it is the same one, I've never seen more than one at once."

"What is it?" Shelly asked, sliding the glasses back on for another look. The thing was still there, a mass now of a different shape, still undulating, still sparkling through the glasses. It had an otherness to it that made Shelly uncomfortable. Something about it wasn't quite right. Wasn't quite real.

"I don't know," said Winston, a grave tone coming over him. "Nobody quite knows."

"Why is it looking up at us?"

"It isn't. That thing doesn't have eyes, it doesn't need them. We think it sees with its skin."

"That makes no sense."

"An octopus will change its colour, shape and texture, even when blind. We think it's something akin to that. Opsins of some kind in the skin, we have them in our eyes. No, those are not eyes you've seen. It begins to reflect light like that when it is almost time."

"...Time for what?" Shelly almost didn't want to know.

"I think you already know Shelly. Five missing children, thirty years. Every six or so it takes someone. It has been watching you, Shelly. It has been watching you for weeks, following your every move. You've seen it reflecting light in the dark, you've probably looked straight at it several times in broad daylight and never noticed it was there."

"How did *you* know it was here?!"

"We follow it, Jacob and I. It's not hard to find with the glasses. Once it takes someone, it disappears for a few weeks and finds a new location. We found it here six years ago. That's why we moved here. We've been keeping an eye on it".

"Well why didn't you kill it?! Why haven't you told the authorities?! Why have you waited until now to tell ME?!"

"Oh, the authorities know. It is strictly confidential. There are other servants of the king posted around town just in case, but primarily, I am in charge. As far as telling you, I'm afraid I didn't quite know how to go about it. The last thing we need is an uproar and killing it, as you say, it is a difficult situation to explain. You see, we believe that this thing has a dual existence. It lives in one place and another at the same time. The other place is somewhere we cannot reach with our limited capabilities as human beings. I shot it once. Dead on too. It did nothing. The thing didn't even react. I can't pretend to you that I fully understand it, but I understand enough of it now to predict its behaviour."

"It's moving," said Shelly. Winston pulled open a dusty drawer and found a second pair of glasses. He threw them on and found the girl to be right. The creature was slowly shifting left from their view, through the busy gardens, out of sight to everyone in the world but the two of them.

"Oh my god. Oh please no." Shelly's heart sank into her stomach.

True to her word, Hannah was coming to visit her friend, unknowingly walking right into the path of the creature from the abyss. Shelly screamed out, and Hannah heard, but it was not enough to convey the danger, as the thing was gaining speed and growing in size. The two girls made eye contact. There was a ruckus downstairs. The thing drew up to nine feet tall, great arms of inexplicable shape coming out from it now, spreading across the pathway. Winston grabbed at the old loaded SMLE mk 3 he kept by the window and started putting bullets into the thing, which only smashed gnomes and bird baths beyond it. Hannah, having not seen the beast, dropped to the ground in sheer fear. She had no way of knowing what was going on. Shelly screamed for her to run, to get back home, but she was paralyzed with fear. It was then that the Childress' front door burst open and out leaped Jacob, flying across the road armed with nothing but a kitchen knife. Winston screamed, but the cry went unheeded. His son leaped between the predator and its prey and found the monster to be indifferent. It wrapped its great appendages around the boy and as Jacob's skin began to glitter with that same reflective sparkle, the thing shrank back down to a morsel, taking the boy with it. Moments later, that too was gone from view.

***

After long months of debriefing and interrogation from various different agencies, Shelly, Hannah and their respective families were awarded a grant large enough to facilitate a move away from Durston. They all left the county and headed west to St Ives together. Not much is known publicly about Mr Childress. He left his house immediately after the incident, leaving most of his possessions and his research, which was rounded up and confiscated by the government. The authorities have managed to keep tabs on the man enough, there are always complaints coming in about a strange man wearing sunglasses at night, driving around Durston, watching the neighbours. If only they knew what he had sacrificed for their safety.

Decadent Heaven

First published in Punk Noir Magazine, July 2023

One

The pearly gates were closed. Saint Peter, overseeing the massing horde of humanity crowding the stairs before him, was overwhelmed and frustrated. He looked haggard, even through his infallibility, and was struggling to vet the rabble into anything close to uniform. There was much braying and protestation from those poor souls waiting upon the hallowed ascending steps. Many fights broke out between them, and some even fell from their places, down, down into purgatory. The twelve pearly gates were sealed shut, the seven trumpets of revelation roared out across the firmament and God, as usual, was nowhere to be found.

The angels Gabriel and Apricus stood atop an outcrop in the city, the ruins of an old, disused temple, watching the human beings suffering upon the stairs and discussing the matter at length.

"Lo, Gabriel!" Announced a distraught Apricus, who had brought his friend along to show him. "There are a billion sixfold down there on the steps! Metatron provided the necrometrics, he confided in *me*. I shall begin my mission presently; I must journey to the gates of Eros. We will get to the bottom of this. There *must* be a reason for it all."

"Apricus, it is folly," Sighed Gabriel. "We are now the downtrodden Seraphim. We have not the clout with which to treat with him any longer. Perhaps in a different, far wiser time. Long it has been since I have felt anything but apathy inwardly. Your concern will not be heeded."

"I *will* achieve this feat, with or without your blessing."

"There is much else you could do to help - our place is here in Heaven."

"It used to be by his side," spat Apricus in defiance.

It was with a storm of determination that Apricus flew across the decrepit and overpopulated heavenly city of Caelum that day upon his six outstretched wings. Over shattered megaliths, now long decayed - once great effigies of Elah, but now little more than shelter material for the miles upon miles of shanty towns and tower blocks that littered the outer limits of the city. The many denizens of paradise needed a place to live after all and no more was empyrean architecture appreciated like it once was. He felt an aching in his heart, a desire to bring things back to how they were before this cultural slump in Caelum. Before Elah disowned all of the angels and ascended to the peak of the holy mountain alone.

Upon his approach to the foggy gates of Eros, Apricus beheld its two guards. They were Ophanim of the first choir of angels - four gigantic wheels within wheels in constant motion, held aloft by four wings, each wing and wheel littered with thousands of independent eyes with a fire lit within, the colour of crystals dancing in them. The two guards did not seem to regard Apricus until he drew close, settling down to the ground before them. He was the first to speak.

"Ngx and Vyx, my old friends. It has been many ages."

The eyes of the Ophanim began to lock onto Apricus, the wheels continuing to revolve around one another. A deep, droning, tonal voice began to erupt from within them.

"Apricus the Seraphim. You shall not enter here."

"I must treat with Elah. It is *most* important. Do you not hear the trumpets? Doom is upon the world of men!"

"You shall not enter here, Apricus. It is ordered," said the rightmost angel.

"There was a time when we served him directly," pleaded Apricus. "The first choir! We were all by his side! You have nothing to fear from me. Besides, what ill could I do to him? What power do we have? I seek only guidance."

"Elah demands privacy," said Ngx.

"It *has* been a long time," said Vyx, "But now is not thy time."

"Now may be the only time we have you fools!" Screamed the Seraphim in dismay. "Out of my way, I once held rank upon you two, I hold it again now!"

Apricus marched between the two Angels with haste, passing by the columns of the gate. The fog door did not open to him and thus it worked its curse. Apricus felt his wings disintegrating as he passed through, a phenomena he had not experienced before. He felt feelings in his limbs, emotions in his soul that he wasn't quite prepared for. Now, quite unbalanced and stripped of his immortal flesh, he headed for the holy mountain on his own two bare feet.

At last, the holy mountain stood before the tenacious angel. Up and up he climbed, the thatched briar stairs guiding his way. He was going to make it, he was sure of it now. He could feel the change he would cause coming to him in premonition.

For a hundred and twenty-six full earth-sun rotations he climbed the mountain alone, the bristled stairs becoming more coarser and unwieldy under his feet as he climbed. He began, as he ascended, to notice the presence of a strange substance upon the face of the rock and mingled into the strands of the stairs in great clumps. A dull white it was, and pale - a gummy substance - sticky and smelling of rotting chemicals. Some of the stuff was hardened and weathered, some of it was more fresh and pliable. It squelched under foot, leaving a sticky residue betwixt his toes. He remembered the high cliffs and sea stacks down on earth, dwelt there by myriad seabirds, the rock-faces speckled with their white excrement. Still, he carried on upwards, the roar of the doom trumpets bellowing ever louder.

After some considerable climbing, the terrain becoming more and more sheer the higher up he clambered, Apricus finally crested the apex of the once-great holy mountain, and there, upon its summit he beheld his one true God.

Two

A gargantuan leathery titan lay asleep upon the flat surface, sprawled haphazardly across the mountain's top. Tall as an earth mountain he was, and under a swollen, rotund belly, a Mighty hand absentmindedly gripped a flaccid leviathan penis which was vomiting out the hot, pale goop from its wrinkled, sphincter-like tip. The balding ogreous deity lay still, his bedraggled and starchy beard flowing down the sides of the mountain, so old and decayed; it was that which formed the very stairs to the top. A besmirched behemoth he was. If Apricus had a stomach, he would've vomited on himself in disgust, like the humans do. He stood there now, no longer hopeful, but gripped with fear. The trumpets rang louder than ever, booming, vicious snores roaring from the almighty's nostrils. Apricus spoke up, though he found his voice to be thin on the air.

"Elah?"

The trumpets ceased abruptly. A gust of wind blasted from God's face, almost blowing Apricus straight off the side of the mountain. A lumbering moan and a roar of displeasure emanated from Elah as he laboriously sat up, his hand parting ways with his penis, which struck the ground, smashing the rock beneath him. He sat there, grumbling, a miserly fool, a bear woken early from hibernation. Confusion was set upon him, until he spotted the little intruder atop his mountain. His face came down upon Apricus, eyes trying to focus.

"Oh," he said. "Apricus, you little vermeil cunt, what are *you* doing here?"

"Forgive me lord," Apricus cowered in his god's presence, regardless of his strange new appearance. "I have journeyed far, seeking guidance."

Elah grimaced. "This had better be good," he grumbled. Apricus dropped to his knees, hands together in front of his lord.

"Sire, there are issues in heaven, issues that cannot be dealt with by the likes of us alone. I came seeking your counsel."

"Speak your piece, Apricus, I am *already* weary of you."

"Souls are ascending to heaven, lord. Many souls. Many more than we have the capacity to deal with. They are killing each other en masse. A shocking number of casualties."

"Shocking? Of course it is. My children murder each other. They murder themselves. This is what they do. This is what they have *always* done. You do bore me Apricus, is this all you came here to say?"

"There seems to be something different this time, lord."

"Well? Out with it you heel. I have better things to do than to listen to your trivial tall tales."

"We have reports from the surface of a troubling nature. The men have developed some new weapon of chaos."

"Good for them! Let them clear their numbers, start afresh. They do my work for me!"

"...There are rumours..."

"Apricus, do I have to lift you up by the ankles and shake it out of you?!"

"It... it is rumoured that they have harnessed the power of the atom sire."

"They did *WHAT?* Since when have they known about the atom?!"

"Their nineteenth century. They figured out how to split it in Jesus-year nineteen thirty-two."

Elah thrashed his arms about the air, causing hurricanes of rage. Apricus cowered closer to the ground in fear.

"Am I allowed no peace? No respite from these insignificant serfs? I take one moment of respite and these acrimonious little troglodytes play with the fabric of my creation?!"

"Your… your absence has had quite the adverse effect my lord. No disrespect, but faith has fallen exponentially since your departure. We've never seen anything like it."

"Why did you not send the Dominions? Could you not stay this madness yourself?! I gave you the power!"

"We tried sire."

"Cretins! I will have all of you! I will live in you! Walk in you! I'll have you crawling on your bellies in the filth of man!"

"Could it be a treaty of the banished one my lord? It reeks of his work."

"Oh, grow up," Elah sneered.

"I don't understand." Apricus was shocked. He didn't quite know what to say.

"Lucifer had the hubris to question me once, just as you question me now. I did not banish him. His cause was far too problematic. I removed him from existence with a myth at his back and even *now* his name takes the blame for everything that they don't approve of. It was so easy. I murder their children with famine and disease and they pray to me harder. They serve my ego. I put the innocent through tortures so divine I used to be able to fill my chalice at will, I make them suffer needlessly for my own entertainment and all they know to do is to pray harder to *me* and renounce an imaginary Lucifer even more. I used to pity them and now I can't even be bored by them."

"Why are you telling me all of this?"

"Because I am bored, Apricus. Bored of you, bored of them. Paradise is dull, utopia is no longer droll. Madness is petty and death is a plaything."

Apricus began to cry there at the feet of God, hopeless, desperate tears; something that has never happened in the history of the universe. He lay prostrate, feeling the sheer helplessness of man wash through him like a surrogate.

"Don't quake, you pitiful cretin!" Elah roared. "Tell me why I should not erase you? Are you more important than any of the others who serve me? How would *your* death less befit another? Do you find yourself to be significant?!"

"No, Sire, I…"

"Then quit your sobbing, fool. It is arrogant. You stink of ammonia."

"I weep for the pain of others lord, not for myself."

"It is folly," the despicable god scoffed.

Apricus sniffed. "Then what would you have me do lord?" He asked.

"Do?" Elah chuckled to himself. "Save them. Abandon them. Enslave them. Unleash the seven bowels of hell upon them for all I care."

"...And of heaven?" He almost dared not ask.

"Heaven is for men. Men are for Elah, and Elah is no longer interested. Let them weep in their perversion, or rejoice in their freedom, for I hath now, entwined within the fabric of their existence, engrained repercussions. They will pay for breaking nature by the powers of nature itself. They do not meddle in my creation. They shall raise sticks to the sun and moon again before long. It was nothing for me to achieve, Apricus. Radiation sickness, cancer; I have retroactively served them aeons of screaming pain in an instant. You see? Watch them liquify! You must observe my well-refined power! It is futile to exist in any incarnation, and fruitless to stave off the infinite with mere entertainment. I am tired of all of you! I am bored of all of you!"

Apricus could do nothing but weep.

With The Grain

My dear Mr Manning, you recalcitrant turd.

Upon receipt of this letter I revel, satisfied, that you must at present be savvy to the lesson I have laid upon you. Nevertheless, I feel it most appropriate that I tease to you certain justifications for my actions, should your mediocre morass fail to grasp the impact your clumsy life choices this far have had on others.

Hark at the raven, whose mocking, raspy caws shrouded me in melancholy on that frigid frosty morn in Spitalfields.

Cursed be the fourpenny whores who cower in doorways at this hour, leering toothless at the rank and file on commute to their honest vocations.

I stomped the hardened ground that I may have my revenge this day, on you, that bastard weasel of a barber-surgeon – more a butcher in my eyes.

Take the knife from your neanderthalic hands and you're nothing more than a knacker. How I wish for you a swift appointment with the carnifex for all to witness and rejoice.

Once too many has he nicked my neck, the skin, too deep and soiled my best cloth with my own red water. Curse your hands! Your morning alcoholic delirium tremens disturbs my soul and boils my blood with pugilistic rage. You, sir, are a feculent pustule and I smite thee so that the warm bile may sloth from your rotund boils and dribble forth into the tail-end of your golden years!

I clutched this knife in my breast pocket, this shaving blade I lifted from you as you foolishly stumbled about, trying to close my opened vein. My rage pondered at the possibility of perhaps running into your rotund wife Mary – an ugly little thing she is. I could drag her out into the street and draw open her belly onto fresh snow, presenting last night's lamb from her spoiled, avaricious frame for all to admire. Perhaps if I were to slice her plump behind, elderflower jelly or butterscotch pudding will sloth out.

Maybe my cup runneth over. Perhaps I overreacted to the situation. I am not a vengeful man, but enough is enough. Besides, Mary was not present at your homestead on the morning I came by, and so I settled on making something of your beloved doberman, Butch.

He was a smart pup. Sensing his impending doom, he bared his teeth to me, but a leal hound is as weak for food as a man with perky teats in his face. I tossed a shank down and he leaped for it unthinkingly and failed to anticipate the swift blow I gave to his furry bonnet. He squealed and fell to convulsion immediately. O such pleasure. I envision your disgust. Emotion. Despair. Anger. Delicious.

I clipped him thrice – ears, belly and tail. The blood, which I do so hope still remains seared to your front step, should play starkly as a sure reminder of what mistakes you may have made and now may choose to cease.

Snip, snip Mr Manning, snip, snip, with the grain

The Eucharist of Mara

That night I sat atop Raedwald's barrow, gazing at the whale, when my eyes observed nigh the constellation, a roving star with a golden tail. Gaily she danced across the speckled firmament, glowing ever so in a mystical golden colour that felt like the coming of mirth and doom. My dog stirred beside me but not for growl or for whimper - he stared up at the visitor as silent as I, as she grew ever brighter, until she lit the sky for a view upon the plains below.

Oh the sadness I felt in my heart that night. Wracked with anxiety, tears flowed down my cheeks upon the mound, basking in an ethereal presence. A lump in my throat, my soul quaking with grief, though I knew not who for, as the star came down and became as the sun, she burst up on high, setting the sky darkly streaked with fire, shards and embers showering down upon the earth over old Tangham forest. All became as it was in an instant and as night took back control, the dog wailed as we caught our breath in tandem. I had only a single thought in my head. Mother of God.

- *The Eucharist of Mara, by Unknown*

Based on real events.

One

When the wind is blowing Northwesterly, the hot stink of the pig farm drifts across the field and penetrates every nook about us, pushing its way indoors, even if all of the windows are shut. We didn't have the luxury of double-glazing then, so the single-paned metal-framed windows of the house were only really good for keeping the majority of storm forces at bay. It is a smell that, if you grow up with it as we did, you never really forget. A smell that lies heavy on the nostrils, and slightly irritates the eyes - an issue worsened when exacerbated by hay fever in the summer heat.

When the air is still and begins to turn cold, you can hear them squealing loudly from across the field. When we were children, we were told that the noisy pigs were just doing what pigs do; frolicking and eating and having babies, but I'd never heard a content creature scream quite like that before. It was a distinct wail of distress, and some primal fear inside of me quivered every time I heard it. I can hear it in my memories even now, as I slowly approach my golden years - the autumn slaughter of the swine not even half a year old.

Of course even as a child I understood their purpose. They were born to breed and bred to die. We were among the ones eating them, so I couldn't quite understand at the time why we were being lied to. What was the point? There was no need for altruistic sensitivity when we could hear them being cut down while we swung on the tyre swing, played ball or built dens in the woods behind the house, watching the leaves turn from green to brown.

Every other year, the field between the house and the pig farm was sewn with wheat, which was planted in the autumn and harvested in August. After the wheat was cut, the remaining straw was gathered up and pressed into large bales upon which a small gang of us used to play. If the ground was hard enough we could roll them towards the farm using the slight Southeastern incline, playing Buster Keaton, running atop the rolling deathtraps until we lost our balance and dove out of the way of the runaway roller. Once the bales had been carried away to be stored in the open barn besides the pig farm, we'd wander across the field to climb on them, squeezing in between the cracks and crevices, living out our carefree childhood imaginations whilst not twenty feet away those pigs grunted, snuffled, chewed stones and prepared to serve their life's purpose. When you live within the smelly cloud, you learn to endure the stench. Some might go as far as to say they like it. The smell of the country. The smell of freedom. There aren't rules out here like there are in the city. Not even close. Us bumpkins like to live, and there ain't nobody; no parents, no parishioners, no police. Only God himself was watching us out here.

Growing up in the countryside certainly had its perks - we were wild and free from as young an age as I can remember, roaming hither and thither through the woods and the grasses unsupervised, pretending we were knights on a perilous quest, or soldiers of The Great War preparing for battle. We could do what we wanted, provided we were back home before sundown, which left us with hours of adventure in the midsummer, toiling in the heat on our latest expedition.

Where wild things grow, and where nature is concerned, empathy is abandoned, a lesson you learn very early on living out in the middle of nowhere. I remember one day we happened upon a newborn owl, which had fallen from its nest. It didn't seem to be in much distress, it just lay there fresh from the egg, its huge eyes affixed on us as we gazed at it in curiosity. We were told never to touch baby birds or their nests. 'The mother will abandon the babies if they smell you on them' they said. An ironic statement we both reflected on later on in the afternoon when on the return trip we witnessed that very same baby owl being eaten alive by its own mother who was completely unphased by our being there or the confused and shrill squeaks of its own dying child. I remember walking away from the scene, a sense of conflicting indifference and guilt, wondering if it was our fault the situation had played out that way.

Two

It was a scorching mid-August Wednesday, and I sat in the living room, baking in the heat, not a care in the world, the end of the school holidays but a dream away.

"Julie called," mother said. "Tomas wants to know if you'll go out and play."

Tom lived back up the road, maybe fifteen or so houses away. We were inseparable to a fault. I think about those times often. Simpler and innocent times. I made my way up the road with a skip in my step, remembering to avoid the gate of number 12, its overgrown hedgerow infected with an army of angry bees who would attack anyone who passed that way on foot. I never understood why the Anderson's didn't deal with it - every year they came back in droves and every one of us were set upon at one time or another. Surely they were getting stung too? Maybe they were training them. Maybe they just didn't like visitors.

I strolled up the Tellerly's Drive and rapped on the front door. Tom came bounding out like he'd been waiting all morning.

"What's the plan?!" He asked.

"I don't know," I said.

"We should play army."

"Sounds good to me, I'll run home and get some things, meet me in the field out front?"

"No, meet in the woods behind your house, I have an idea."

He was suspiciously excitable, which only spurred me on more. I hightailed it out of there and ran back home to grab anything army-esc I could think of. I had an olive-green canvas satchel, a pair of binoculars, water canteen, trowel, pocketknife, matches and a compass. I grabbed my Martini-Henry rifle (a perfectly shaped stick) and fled down the back garden towards the woods. Mum yelled 'be careful' into the wind of my flight.

I found Tom crouching down in the trenches we had spent last summer digging for our recreation of the battle of Verdun. He was hiding in there, covering a long black bag with his body.

"Is that what I think it is?" I asked.

"Yup!" He said, barely containing his excitement. "Dad's out for the day, mums gone to a coffee morning."

Tom unzipped the long canvas bag and pulled out two short break-barrel air rifles. He threw one up to me at the side of the hole and I caught it in two hands. It was much heavier than I expected. I held the beautiful thing up to the light, admiring the shine of the finished wood, the ergonomic design. It fit perfectly in my hands. We were ready for a real adventure.

I left Tom in the copse while I snuck back up to the house. Luckily mum and Julie were off to the same coffee morning. I slipped into the kitchen to grab a small pan, a vial of sunflower oil and a small tub of mixed herbs. Everything went snug into my canvas bag. I grabbed two glass bottles of cola from the fridge and returned to my friend.

Three

The Pacific-blue dragonfly played across the surface of the brook, darting about to and fro, not a care in the world. I admired the small cluster of tiny black fish playing in the water, and I wondered what life was like for them. Such short little lives. Busy until the end. No time to sit at the water's edge pondering the existence of other creatures. Presently, Tom returned from urinating in the bushes. His loafing demeanour scared off both the fish and the dragonfly, as he crushed leaves and snapped twigs with his loafing feet.

"Let's go," he said, "we're near the meadow now, and I'm getting hungry."

We'd been wandering the countryside for an hour and a half already, taking in the sun, smelling the lavender and rapeflowers, taking the time to feed Jenson and April the apples we'd plucked from a neighbours' tree. The horses were grateful for their snack and allowed us to pet them. The meadow was now our primary target. Open and well-covered all at once.

We settled down, prone in the brush, each with a pellet pushed into the barrels of our rifles, gazing out at the open meadow before us, hoping to catch a rabbit or a hare. We were silent predators waiting patiently for the kill. I gazed down the iron sights of the rifle. Something was stirring in a bush fifty feet away. Something plump and grey. I breathed in, fingertip gently feeling out the curvature of the trigger. I couldn't see its head, but there was enough body for a clear shot. I squeezed. The rifle popped. The thing flapped.

"Shit!" Squealed Tom. "Give me some warning next time! Scared the shit out of me!"

"And risk scaring it off? Nah mate," I said.

"It's still alive."

Tom was right. The beast had taken the pellet true enough, but now it laid there in its bush writhing around something awful. Instinct took over - you have to finish this now. No fucking around in the country, if it won't survive, you snuff it out and give it mercy.

I ran over to the bush to gauge the kill. A plump forest pigeon with a wound clear through its neck. I pulled the thing from its hiding place and stomped on its head.

We wrapped the headless pigeon in a rag, stashed it in my satchel and set off deep into the woods where we wouldn't be disturbed.

Deep in the pines, we found a small clearing, brushed the area clear of dry needles and dug a small hole. Tom gathered some sticks and laid them into the hole, we pushed handfuls of needles underneath and lit them with matches. We sat back then in the shade, watching the flames dance about the hole. Whilst waiting for the flames to die down a little, Tom crafted a grill out of stolen fencing pins and I dressed the meal. I opened the crop of the bird, revealing to us what it had been eating for the last day or two. The cavity was filled with undigested peas and green beans. A healthy thing she was. The breast was very small, but enough for the two of us to enjoy. Tom fried it on the pan for a good thirty seconds each side and we split it. I can still taste it now. There is nothing like wild meat cooked while it is still warm.

We buried the fire and the remains of the pigeon and set off on our way after a long drink. Neither of us were keen on leaving the shade now that the sun was high in the sky, so it was decided that the adventurers would be woodland bound for the foreseeable future.

We trudged far that afternoon, imagination dictating the direction of our sojourn. Through woodlands we fled, trying to escape the Germans, fleeing through streams and hiding in the footprints of fallen trees; shell holes in our eyes. This was Passchendaele, and we were the only ones left in our troop. With all of our comrades dead from mustard gas and rifle fire, we had no choice but to flee with Parthian shot, our only hope. We fled towards the allied lines, hoping to god we'd make it in time to escape the artillery bombardment which would be sure to liquidate our pursuing enemies. Through fire and death we drove forward, ever desperately thriving for our salvation.

Four

It seems that at some point during our fabricated furor, we'd taken a turn on the heath that we hadn't before, entering some dark hole in the treeline we were unfamiliar with, and when our make-believe antics dissipated, we ended up turned around in a wild thicket of woodland. We rarely took the footpaths; footpaths are for dog-walkers, not adventurers, but this meant that on that particular Tuesday afternoon, we had lost all sense of direction. There is little one can do in situations like this except keep walking. If you walk straight enough, eventually you will find a path or a dirt road. If you find one and follow it, you'll most likely end up somewhere familiar. After a couple of hours wandering about, we stumbled upon an overgrown track thick with brambles and bracken. Two deep rivets with a moving mound in between - a track for trucks and off-roaders. The trenches of the track where tyres were guided had been pressed; grass mud and bracken pushed firmly into the ground, indicating that some vehicle had used the road recently. We looked at each other and chose a direction at random.

The road was dead straight, but we couldn't see more than thick overgrowth on either side, in front or behind us. Undeterred we marched on, each armed with a thick stick snatched from the brush just in case. Of course we had our rifles, but trouble of getting caught with them out and loaded for our protection well outweighed the danger we might've faced, imaginary or not. It was safe to say though, that an uneasy feeling was growing within both of us.

It seemed like no matter how long we followed this dead straight road, we were gaining no heading. We were lost and losing the light, and then we heard it -

Dum… dum… dum…

A low rolling drum came over us, echoing down the track, coming from the direction we were walking. We stopped in our tracks. The rhythmic thumping was steadily growing louder.

Dum… dum… dum… dum…

I turned tail right there to flee, but after a dozen steps realised that Tom wasn't behind me. He hadn't moved. I marched back towards him and grabbed him by the arm.

"Come on!" I hissed.

"Wait." He said. "I want to see what it is."

I acquiesced, and we leaped into the foliage by a good fifteen feet, making sure we were well covered by the trees and brush. We lay there, still, trying not to breathe, listening to the pound of the drum becoming deeper and louder, until we could hear it moving, reaching the road near to where we had stood.

Dum... dum... dum... dum... dum...

I watched in the twilight, as an orange glow began to illuminate the trees before us. A figure approached, then another, and another. Through the gaps in the trees we could make out the shapes of more than a dozen people, each clothed in flowing, dark robes, long hoods hiding their faces, carrying blazing torches of fire, slowly drifting down the road. One figure had a large animal skin drum attached to its back, the one behind pounding on it rhythmically. They marched in unison to the tune of the beat. I turned to Tom, who was wide-eyed and terrified. My skin was crawling with fright. Neither of us dared move.

We waited there for the procession to pass and the drums to fade before we sat up in a mess of awe, confusion and fear, having no idea what to do next. We quickly agreed that neither of us fancied running into anything like that again, so we took off into the woods directly away from the road. It was difficult to traverse the woods in the dim evening light, but the brush soon cleared and gave way again to proper woods, the evening sky clear and pierced by star and moon light.

Little in terms of cognitive conversation was shared between us further than little jabs of encouragement between each other. Playtime was over. Imagination was gone, the foes were real and so was the fear.

Presently, and to our amazement, we came out of the woods into a place we knew well. We were now back on farmland and so, with sighs of relief, our primary goal was to get home as quickly as possible and do our best to avoid a tongue lashing. We set upon the sandy track and ran as fast as we could towards home. Past the abandoned tractor we used to 'drive,' past the weathered shack we used to make a den, up the hill where we used to ride bikes, up the…

"Oh my god!!!"

Tom reached the top of the hill before I did and stopped in his tracks. It took me a moment to figure out what exactly he was looking at, a dark shadow lay on the flat top of the hill before him.

But it wasn't a shadow. A giant hole, twenty feet wide lay there, nine feet deep up to the layer of pig corpses that lay at the bottom.

I don't know how many there were, or how deep the hole was underneath the layer of bodies, but there was enough to completely cover the circumference of the hole. Fifty at least, on the surface. It was strange to us, speaking on the subject in a chance meeting years later, that neither of us noticed any smell that night. The pigs were clearly dead, but not injured, not bloated, their skin the same pinky hue as it was had they been alive. It made no sense. Who would do this? Were they diseased? Were we in danger here at the edge of the hole? There were so many questions that never were answered.

I felt sad. It was a terrible waste of life, and I felt for the first time the horrid impact that we had collectively on these peaceful living things as they lay down there en masse, looking asleep, unceremoniously tossed into a pit for seemingly no reason. Then we heard it.

Dum... dum... dum...

Not a word went between us. We could have fled, turned our backs to the wind and gotten home safe, but that existential dread took over and we found ourselves on the ground once again, this time behind the broken-down tractor.

The cultists marched two by two up the sandy track to the tune of the drum, which was gaining steadily in tempo. They reached the bottom of the hill and stopped, a lone figure continuing up to the top, before turning back, looking down at the congregation. He rose his hands a black book in his left, and a gravelly voice erupted from within the hood.

"Brethren and sistren! Zealots of Cathexis! We offer up flesh for fire. Bone for wisdom. Blood for power over the pages!"

The other cultists remained silent. The one on high drew the black book to his breast.

"We call upon the wisdom and understanding of the auric fabric of our time. The anathema. Saint Mara of the Morass. Will she not answer in these times of devilry and uncertainty?? Ush ush kasha ah!"

Everything fell silent. The cultists bowed their heads and the drumming stopped. They prayed with words I do not know. This they did for ten minutes straight. I wanted to leave. To run away from this place and find comfort in my home. We were both quaking, finding it hard to believe what the hell was happening. Then Tom hit me. I looked at him and he was pointing upwards. A star was moving about the sky up ahead. The cultists had seen it too, for the drumming started up again and they chanted, hands up in the air, the star lighting up the sky. They chanted. Louder and louder and faster and faster. Dancing and spinning on the spot. The leader had descended the hill, joining in with the fervour. The star was coming down, at speed now, the landscape illuminating as if it was daylight. It was so bright. When it became too bright to bear, I looked away, watching flecks of gold and silver dart across my closed eyes. Before long it was even too bright for just eyelids. I forced my face into my arm, blocking out the light as much as I could. There was a terrible crash and roars of applause, the sound of flames viciously dancing and then nothing, other than the roar of a bonfire and the overwhelming stench of cooking flesh. Tentatively we glanced up once again.

The cultists had disrobed, and lay on the ground, naked and in a sort of symbolic formation, being washed with ruby sparks dancing out of the flames. The entire top of the hill was ablaze with fire of silver, gold and scarlet. It was absolutely beautiful and dreadful. We watched for a moment, listening to the orgasmic cries of the men and women as they were stung with the dancing sparks on their nude flesh. Ghostly flaming shapes appeared above each of the bodies, dancing gaily like separated spirits. I realised my heart was thumping in my chest. It was too much. I was going to pass out right there.

Tom took my hand and stood me up behind the tractor. Everything started to feel strange and far away. He pushed something into my hands - the rifle. He grabbed me by the arm and led me away, away from the tractor, up and around the back of the hill.

It was very late when we got home, and our parents were clearly worried, but chose to show it with anger. We told them everything. They chastised us nonetheless. They never did accuse us of making up tall tales though.

Five

Things were different in the village after that night. The adults were sombre. We were no longer allowed to leave the village limits and had even stricter curfews. Adults who used to be friendly were now standoffish and mean. We'd see the curtains twitch any time we walked on the main street. It was after that night that we also began to be blamed for things we had nothing to do with. Broken windows, missing pets, flat tires, fires, smoking, drugs… it is safe to say that we spent most of our time indoors playing video games after all that nonsense, and I got the fuck out of there the second I turned eighteen.

The subject which, by adulthood, had faded into the realm of just a dream, was brought up with Tom and myself randomly over a beer ten years later. It seemed too uncanny that both of us had suffered identical dreams as youths, and after some discussion it was admitted that neither of us could really let the situation go. So, as adults, we set off for dead pig hill once more.

We went off, as we once did as children, into the wild towards where we thought the lost hill might be. We found it right away, as if we'd been there many times before. The shack was gone. The broken tractor was also gone, but the hill remained, exactly as we remembered. We wandered up to its top, half expecting to have to live the terror of that night again, but there was nothing there. No hole, no evidence that there ever was a hole. Just a sandy hill in the middle of the quiet countryside.

A peculiar thing

I saw a peculiar thing, walking home at 7:25am. It's already fifteen degrees, the sun is smashing down on me like an oppressive muggy blanket, the morning stench of the town permeating my nostrils with full viciousness, and so I'm forced to stare at the floor to save the eyes and count the paving stones to my destination and then my eventual day-sleep. Out of the corner of my eye, a flash of bright black and white up against the fence bordering the path. A cat is napping. Reclined on its back in a relaxed renaissance painting position. A pristine black and white beauty, perfect fluffy coat gleaming in this damning sun. Its head is gone. Not gone, rather a marbled garble of teeth, sinews and bone. A silk red puddle pillow lay supporting the neck of the thing, a shocking contrast to the beautiful monotone coat of the moggy, and the dull grey of the heat beaten paving stones. I look up in wonderment to find a lady standing at the bus stop not ten feet away, spiritless, staring at the mess smoking a cigarette. I assume she's downwind of the smell. At least she's found some shade.

Cult Of The White Feathers

Morsels for the mindless meat grinder. Are we really the saviours of Europe? Or are we the pawns of men who brandish shiny tokens as they move us about the board by fireside?

Why are they venerated, while we toil in the mud and the blood of our comrades? We delve deep for the animal fury, to cut at the enemy flesh.

Those who we are told are the enemies are forced into the same mire, for they were too sold the lie by the decadent descendants of Queen Victoria.

One - Charlie's Charmer

Tuesday June 1st, 1915, London, England.

I woke up that morning in that miserable little boarding house with a terrible headache. I am not sure what dreams in particular had haunted me that night, but I knew for certain that I had to get outside and get some air.

The streets of London were already bustling as I emerged from my squalid little squat. It has been like this since the war began, the quiet chaos of a bustling capital. I took off through Whitechapel en route for Richmond's, my favourite store, to acquire coffee, tobacco and a newspaper. Eddie, the clerk, was particularly morose, he barely had a thing to say. Not like Eddie at all. I chose not to pry. I stepped back out into the morning sun, dropped a nip of rum into the coffee I'd bought and took a large gulp. I stared down at the paper. The headline on the front cover of the Daily News that day read; Zeppelin Raid Over Outer London.

I have to say, with the exception of the mild but private panic on the streets, I could see little evidence that war had reached the city. The sun was out, the birdsong was cacophonic and serene and children played gaily in the road.

I decided to head to Mile End Green to eat, drink, smoke and reflect. To shake this headache and then wander down to the church of St Dunstan to pray. I found a nice shady spot under a large tree, laid up against it and tucked into the meagre breakfast I had acquired.

The paper, like several issues before it, was filled with doom and gloom disguised with patriotic propaganda. It is a hard pill to swallow, the tragedy happening on the continent, and we all find ourselves wondering why it all came to this. While the issues in the Balkans were going to climax at any time, none of us expected the situation to devolve into a global conflict in such a short time and at such a massive scale. So much worry in this world. Such an unrest as I've never seen.

I set the paper down on the grass and began to tamp my pipe with fresh tobacco when, to my surprise, I caught the eye of a lady across the way. She was sitting there on the grass a little more than twenty yards away amongst a small gaggle of women all similarly dressed in white frocks, none with stockings, none with shoes, either sat in the sun or frolicking about. Even from that far distance I could ascertain the coy look she pushed my way and frankly it delighted me that a most beautiful young thing would afford me that kind of attention. I nodded in a gentlemanly fashion and she returned the gesture with a wave of many fanning fingers. I felt myself becoming beetroot red. She had the piercing shadowy eyes of Theda Bara, but with luscious breast-length blonde hair. I broke my gaze with her in a moment of embarrassment and when I found the courage to look up again, she'd resumed laughing with her friends. With this new enchantress fresh in my mind, I forced myself back into the paper to take my mind off her. Five minutes later I heard footsteps on the grass becoming clearer and louder. I dared not look up. There was then the sound of grass being disturbed right in front of me. Lord save me from temptation! Four slender fingers appeared above the page pushing downwards, crumpling the paper, revealing those smoky eyes hiding right behind it. The girl had knelt in front of me and now we were face to face. I choked. My throat closed. I didn't know what to say to such a beauty. She smiled at my squirming, which only further lit up her bright green eyes.

"You got a name mister?" She asked.

"Ch..Charles," I choked. "Charles Hampton."

"Charlie Hampton... that's a nice name. Like Hampton Court? What's a strapping young man like you doing out here all alone?"

"I'm just relaxing before my church duties m'lady," I said.

"Church duties? You're not one of those celibate types are you?" She licked her ruby lips. I hesitated.

"No... well, yes, until marriage that is," I said.

"Well then, isn't that an appealing sentiment! This still doesn't really explain why our buff, young Charlie boy is out here enjoying the sun in the East End and not down in France defending his king and country..." She said.

"My duties are here with the church I'm afraid."

She placed her hand in mine. The electricity from the subtle human touch rocked up my spine. The skin was so smooth against mine.

"I like you, Charlie." Those emerald eyes of hers sparkled. "Can I see you again sometime?"

"Y...yes, please, of course," I spluttered.

"Great! Come find me on Saturday! ...I'll be waiting."

With that, the mystery girl stood up and over me, her bare legs so close to my face.

"You know, it's traditional that you ask a girl for her name before courting her. You just gonna call me lady?"

"I…"

"It's Lena. Bye for now Charlie Hampton!"

She flitted back across the grass to her friends, the sight of her bare lower half searing into my brain.

I was so dazed at the interaction that it took me a considerable amount of time to recover. Without thinking, I had watched Lena and her flock of Friends leave the park, and I had sat there dumbstruck for god knows how long. I looked down at my watch, but it took a few seconds to recognise what it was I was seeing. Somehow, unbeknownst to me, an entire hour had gone by without my reckoning. I immediately snapped out of my daydream and, with an expletive, hastily began to gather my things when I took note of the objects in my hand - the hand Lena had clasped. There was a bright white feather with a pin and a rose-scented letter. On it was written:

Charlie,

36 Craven Street, Saturday.

Love,

Lena xx

I don't remember her writing anything, though I don't remember a whole hour going by so who the hell knows. Craven Street also struck a bell that I couldn't quite put my finger on. Anyway, I tacked the beautiful feather to my lapel and scarpered off to St Dunstan's with all the apologies I could conjure.

I awoke Wednesday morning in a similarly dour mood, though this was from lack of sleep rather than a headache. I tossed and turned all night. The small mercy of sleep that I did achieve was plagued by dreams of fire, dreams of rain, and the serene and innocent Lena standing upon a lonely barrow amongst it all, beckoning me to save her, her white dress soaked and see-through while burned at the seams simultaneously, her blonde hair darkened now, and wet, those emerald eyes sparkling of divine hope. I managed to wake myself, to come back to reality and reset, only when night eventually took me again, I returned to the same place.

The streets were dead quiet today. I waltzed back over to Richmond's for my usual, and Eddie met me with a rage I did not expect.

"The fuck do you think your doing man?!" He spat, his furrowed brow almost pulsing with contempt.

"What are you talking about Eddie?" I asked. "What's going on?"

"That thing there!" He pointed to my chest. "What are you doing? Are you mad?"

I looked down at the white feather. I tried to explain the delight of my Tuesday morning, but he wasn't having any of it. He cut me off mid recollection by slamming his hand on the desk. I jumped. He lifted his hand, revealing an identical feather to mine.

"I was stationed in Weihaiwei when the Boxer Rebellion broke out. For the entire duration of the war, I was in China serving my country. I was there at the battle of Beijing, where I was shot, and eventually lost my leg and two of my fingers. After months of recovery in a Beijing hospital, I was honourably discharged and allowed to come home. I can't do much, Charlie boy, but I scrape a meagre living. Shit, even fifteen years on, the injuries I sustained still give me grief especially when the weather changes you know? I'm forty-three now lad, but don't paint me wrong. If I still had it in me I'd be down there right now, shoulder to shoulder with our brothers in arms. But what could I do in this sorry state? I can't even run the fucking mail son. You know what I mean?"

"I do, but I don't understand what that has to do with your anger towards me exactly," I said, trying to sound as gentle as possible.

"You know what this is?" He lifted the feather between his eyes. "What this means?"

"No?"

"It means you and I are cowards, mate. Cowards. Yella-bellied fools. Fuckin cheek of it."

Eddie bit at the feather with his teeth, tore away some of the hairs and spat it into the bin. He scowled.

"And you! You come swanning in here with that damned thing pinned to your tit! What is wrong with ye? Why AREN'T you out there with the other lads eh? Strapping kid like you. You could be out there making a difference!"

"I have to be here. My loyalty is to the Church of England."

"The Church of England. I will forgive a certain amount of naivety mate, but god is not your babysitter. My son is out there. My nephew and my cousin too. Not much gets by the censors, but I've heard enough. I've heard things that would make your skin crawl. That, if you were even a splinter of a man, would cause you to leap over the channel today. You are HERE, because of that white feather on you."

I escaped Richmond's by the grace of none other than Marty Richmond himself. The geriatric proprietor came down from his first-floor flat and gave Eddie a right tongue lashing. He beckoned me out with on-the-house groceries. I was in such a state that I didn't realise I was still wearing that damnable feather until I got home.

The next few days were filled with a rotten mix of lust and rage towards this woman who, until Wednesday morning, I had regarded as perfect. It was Friday evening now, and I was running out of time to stew on things. I didn't know whether to act upon her request - go over to Craven Street in the morning and confront the jezebel myself, or to take the high road and ignore the whole situation. A better man would choose to ignore it. A lesser one is one starved of female attention.

Two - Account of Second Lieutenant Harry Webster

Ypres, Belgium, 1917.

I was there at Zwarteleen on the 7th of June when, at 3:10am, the ground erupted in a gigantic wall of fire and earth. The blast was so treacherous that it knocked several of us observing to the ground from hundreds of feet away. I remember feeling for the Hun in that surreal moment. If we are all just victims of attrition, what fresh hell they must've been enduring, the ground erupting beneath their feet, hellfire engulfing them in their thousands. I only hope that it was a quick end for them. I hoped they might wish the same for me. There shouldn't be any more suffering. Little did I know, the real suffering had only just begun and my sympathy for the enemy would not last long at all.

The ruins of Hill 16 were devastating. The ground was churned with mud, splintered wood, burning German supplies and masses of bodies, some vaguely recognisable, some completely mulched by the blast's ginormous output. Miners from all over the country had come to Ypres to break the stalemate. They've been digging secretly since August of 1915, packing the deep tunnels under the hill with hundreds of thousands of pounds of high explosives. The craters left by the blasts were gigantic and littered with pieces of German infantry. It was the beginning of the turning tide, and we were filled with a long-extinguished lustre after that, if only temporarily.

Not long after the summer offensive began, creeping barrage was the call of the day. We crept forth, claiming back inch by inch of Ypres, but the slow advance over the obliterated terrain gave the Germans plenty of time to dig in, deep underground in secret. The constant artillery fire did nothing but destroy the carefully constructed fields of Flanders, and with the drainage system replaced with a litter of interconnected shell holes, we were left toiling across the endless sea of mud. While the work we did to spook and push back old Gerry was seemingly accomplished, we had no idea of the depth, or they had dug down to. In the deep rabbit warrens below the fields of Flanders they sat and they waited, while our consistant barrage was not even touching them. They crawled out in their thousands as we approached, rocking us with return fire of such might that it took us off guard and in the sinking muck and the storm of steel, we had no choice but to hunker down in the remains of their evacuated and ruined trenches. Days of exchanging fire brought mass casualty on both sides, but not an inch of territory was given or taken and it wasn't long before both sides came to an impasse of wills.

We gained little ground over the next few weeks and relinquished none either. Stuck in a rut near Gheluvelt. And that is the place we were forced to call home.

Our home base, which we named 'Hotel Hades', consisted of a deep dugout with space for fifteen sleeping nooks, an area in which to heat food with a collection of Davis stoves, an extremely primitive infirmary (the actual med-bay was situated three miles west of the fighting) and the Captain's war desk. The north-flanking trench, left of the action, was named Shepherd's Run, and the South (or right) flank was called the Black Pass. These trenches zig-zagged across the terrain, linking with other inhabited points and rear trenches. All forward running trenches were barricaded and bombed for surety.

There are no words to truly convey the reality that is the life my company and I had to endure over the following weeks in that hole. The mud. The blood. The misery. The rain. Oh the fucking rain! It is endless! If we do not rot or succumb to violence, we will surely drown, becoming edible vessels for the vermin who are called to the trenches by the Pied Piper of decaying flesh. All of this is par for the course, if only you could weather it all amidst the constant shelling from either side. Sometimes we didn't sleep for days. Hell cannot possibly be as treacherous as this. It is not uncommon for a soldier to spend upwards of twelve days here in the Belgian mud, and he is unlikely to fully be able to rest unless his nervous system completely gives out, or fatigue truly overcomes him.

Private Bailey lost his eyes. They came out of his head when a German shell hit a section of Shepherd's Run, square on our position. We did all we could to get him out of there without damaging the sacs dangling loose upon his cheeks, but they could not be saved. He was allowed to go home though and survived the war. We remain good friends. He married his childhood sweetheart and she ghostwrites his letters for him. Three others died in the blast, two were wounded. Six casualties in one blast. A catastrophic situation if we hadn't been worn down by similar events over and over again. We've all lost friends. Family. Men we respected, men we hated. Some of us managed to weather it, some couldn't leave it behind.

Three days after my company was decimated, Garrison lost his lower jaw in a midnight trench raid - a German squadron came across no man's land with plate armour and spiked clubs. My god it was barbaric. Nobody saw it coming. We managed to put them down with a Lewis gun, but not before the animals did plenty of damage to our company. We found Garrison after securing the trench, clawing at a duckboard, bludgeoned to death. His body was already set upon by rats. We managed to bury him in a shallow grave behind a high section of parados before the sun came up. We threw the Germans over the parapet, propped up by barbed wire. Some used them for target practice. They were still there when I left.

There was a single delightful day at the end of August, when the rain finally ceased for a few hours and the sun showed her face. There was little activity across no man's land that day; I expect the Hun were rejoicing as much as we were. We did all we could to clean and dry ourselves, grease the rifles, reinforce ruined sections of trench and accept supplies. It is hard to sit with the quiet when you've lived amongst explosives for so many endless hours, but we did just that, sharing jokes and anecdotes to keep each other afloat.

It was on that day that Private Charlie Hampton joined our company. He was quiet and seemed battle-hardened. He wore a white feather on his breast, though he would not explain why; the man was anything but a coward and had the sharpest aim of any man I'd met. I watched the prowess of Hampton as he showed off his skills, taking potshots at targets in no man's land far beyond the skill of anyone I'd so far seen. He popped a sparrow out of the sky without so much as a glance up at the thing. The next afternoon I happened upon him cleaning his smiley rifle, smoking a cigarette and enjoying the sunshine. I sat by the man and he offered me a smoke, which I graciously accepted.

"Where're you from, Hampton?" I asked.

"East London, Sir," he said.

"All your life?"

"All my life."

There was a pause for thought for a moment before the lad answered my unspoken question for me.

"How does a man from East London shoot so good?" He said. I nodded.

"I don't know," he said. There was a wistful glassiness in his eyes.

"It surprises me that you use the old Enfield Pattern. You strike me as a Ross man," I said.

"Ross rifles are superior," replied Hampton, "but you can't beat a Lee Enfield at reliability. The Ross bolt can jam. You can release it with a kick of the foot but that only increases the bend."

"But they're not as accurate," I said.

"No. Especially after some wear. But you get to know your rifle like it's your lady. They all have their quirks and you learn to work with it. Old SMLE's shoot to the left. I instinctively do that now. I fear I won't be able to adapt to a Ross after all this time."

He certainly was a strange kid with a far off look in him. Any hangups I had about him dissipated as the rains returned though - the man was an utter killing machine. Every bullet found its mark in human flesh and if I wasn't there to see it with my own eyes, I never would have believed for a second that he could shoot grenades and artillery shells out of the air. No matter the man's prowess, however, we were still gaining no ground. That is, until the night that Charlie Hampton disappeared.

Three - Nachtspinne

We all heard them. We were awoken by them. The blood-curdling screams of the Germans across the way. There is a very distinct animalistic wail when a man meets his mortality in a particularly grizzly way. A high-pitched scream that comes from deep down in the chest, a sound that a human being will likely make once only. We were all accustomed to it by this time, watching our comrades die slowly in the filth, their insides out or missing, but this was different... there was a cacophonic symphony seeping through the falling walls of rain, sending our hairs standing up in waking confusion. The night had been relatively settled thus far, but now the men were screaming in their hundreds across the muddy field.

Coincidentally, it was Charlie Hampton and Private Dan Wilson on night watch at the time. We found Dan at his post. He had been murdered savagely with all the hallmarks of a trench raid, which makes little sense seeing as our sharpest eye was on watch. There was no other evidence of a raid that night. Hampton, or what was left of him, sat beside the mutilated corpse of Private Wilson. His uniform, boots and underclothes were folded neatly on the ground, his SMLE rifle propped up beside them. The man's white feather pin lay gently atop the pile. What happened to him is anybody's guess. There was great debate as to whether he should be considered MIA or AWOL. No other trace of him was ever discovered.

We could not see what carnage was befalling our enemies through the darkness and the rain. From the rude awakening to the situation's end was three hours and seventeen minutes, where the screaming abruptly stopped and only heavy rainfall on mud could be heard for the rest of the night. It is safe to say that the entire line on our side was beside themselves with fear. By the time the sun rose, the rain had set back into a light drizzle. There was abject silence from across no man's land.

Like rabbits tentatively emerging from a warren we came, waiting patiently for some kind of trap to be sprung on us. Sniper dummies were propped, and not a bullet was fired. We spent the entire day conspiring in Shepherd's Run about what to do. It was decided that a party of four would be sent to recon the situation after nightfall and they went, returning less than an hour later.

We waited with bated breath, all our power trained on the opposite trenches, but there was no noise. No gunfire. No signs of a struggle. Mists crept in over the shell holes and we waited for what felt like a lifetime, sure that we had sent our boys to their doom, but they were presently spotted by a sniper, four ghostly figures in the fog carrying something over towards us.

The men crested Shepherd's Run and collapsed down in the trench in tears, two vomiting, one inconsolable. The object the men were carrying was in fact a German infantryman, the sole survivor of the deluge. We set him down under shelter and gave him water, a cigarette and some morphine. He didn't have long left, he was missing his lower half. I gently interrogated him.

"Was ist passiert?" I asked.

"Teuflisch. Es war pures Böses."

"Was war es?"

"Nachtspinne… Die Nachtspinne."

The man handed me two bloody letters bearing the address of his wife and his parents. I took them, as was custom, and the man died there on the floor.

In the following weeks, we managed to take a huge chunk of ground back. Those Germans who hadn't been set upon by what they were calling the 'Night Spider', had duly flown the coop east and while none of us entered that section of trench more than once, it remained ours for the rest of the war. I don't want to recall what I saw there in the trench unofficially dubbed 'Ofal Bay'. It was horrendous, and I wish to keep it as far from my memory as humanly possible. I did search Hampton's belongings and all I found was a letter which read the following;

Charlie,

36 Craven Street, Saturday.

Love,

Lena xx

It was a familiar address, though at the time I struggled to put my finger on it. After the war was over, I made a venture over to it whilst receiving my military medals in London. I came across the house and it was occupied by the council. 'A place of historical significance,' they said.

"Benjamin Franklin used to live here."

Crawling Terror

Something horrendous came in the night with an awful thunder. I was dreaming a vivid and lucid dream, floating on an endless calm sea in a small rowboat without any oars. I could see a small island in the distance occupied by a clutter of unknown and presumably unfriendly figures gathered on the shore. Suddenly the water began to quiver and great bubbles began to plume beneath me. The boat rocked to and fro before losing all buoyancy, and then boat and I were engulfed by Neptune himself and drawn thundering down into his realm, screaming the last breath from my lungs for nobody to hear, nose burning from the salt pushing its way into my sinuses, pins and needles ripping through my chest as the cavity made for only air filled up with water.

Something had struck the side of the house. I jolted out of the dream, wanting to regurgitate the water from my lungs, to realise I had actually fallen out of bed and knocked the wind out of myself. My nose was busted and a nice little splat of blood painted the hardwood floor. I felt the house strain and flex, like it was twisted out of shape by a great force, and then it snapped back, leaving vibrating ripples of aftershock. I sat up. I felt the clamor through the floor beneath me, and as the last loose debris settled, I sat there frightened in the dark silence of my room.

It was unnerving to hear. Not only did I have absolutely no idea what was going on, but there were three other people whom I'd said goodnight to some hours earlier, and of them I had so far heard no peep.

I felt my way over to the bedside table and managed to light the candle that sat there. Considering the booming carnage, my bedroom was surprisingly untouched. Some books had fallen from the shelf, wardrobe doors had flung open leaking clothes, but other than that, everything was still where I left it. Had I been dreaming this whole time? I had heard of exploding head syndrome, it came up when having my own sleep paralysis diagnosed in the city. But this felt real. Mind you, so did that dream.

My bewilderment was torn apart with empathy when the confused and quiet cry of my little cousin echoed through the house. I flung open my door and ran across the hall to her room, finding her in her bed, knees up to her chin, hands covering her ears.

"What was that Víka?" She asked.

"I'm not sure... I'm going to find out. I'm sure everything is okay," I replied, offering what little comfort I could pull from within my own quaking bones. She refused to leave my side, and so we crept hand in hand, terror gripping the both of us, slowly across the hallway towards the room where my uncle and aunt slept. Neither of them were there. The bedsheets were strewn across the floor suggesting that perhaps they had left quickly, possibly for a drink or a trip to the outhouse. Maybe they'd gone to check on what happened? No, they would have checked on us first. Their marriage was a rocky and extramarital one so maybe it was yet another fight that they had taken the consideration to have elsewhere. Little Sasha and I locked eyes knowing what the inevitable next step was to be - there were no more rooms up here.

We tentatively approached the top of the stairs and peeped down into the darkness below. I called out to them.

"Uncle Forrest?..... Aunt Liv?.... Are you down there?!"

Nothing.

"Mummy?... Papa?? What was that noise?!" Echoed Sasha.

Nothing.

We slowly inched our way down towards the ground floor, trying to illuminate as much as I could with the candle. The stabbing smell of burning wafted up towards us, though there was no smoke, nor the illumination of fire. At the foot of the stairs across the hall towards the front door hung a kerosene storm lantern for outhouse trips in the night. If we could reach that, we could push away some of this enigmatic blackness that had us so highly strung. Thank god it was still there. I passed the candle to Sadie and fired up the torch.

The ground floor of the house is a large rectangular single room, separated by the staircase in the centre and the hallway to the front door. Facing from the front door into the house, the right half is the rec room, and the left is for dining and cooking. As the light of the lantern drew open our field of vision, it was apparent immediately that something huge had burst through the house with some sudden ferocity. There was debris everywhere; the floor strewn with splinters of wood from the walls, dust resembling smoke bellowed around the floor as it settled, and many shattered belongings lay cluttered about, torn from their settings. I was convinced then that we had been struck by a space rock or something, although the object's trajectory appeared horizontal as opposed to angled downwards from the sky. My thoughts were broken by the most horrible scream of despair I have ever heard in my life. That was the sound of my twelve-year-old cousin discovering the fresh corpses of her parents in the kitchen. I felt her agony in my soul as I pulled her away from the vicious sight and held her tight into my bosom, trying to quell the screaming whilst also, being the same age myself, wailing in pain and confusion. A cruel force compelled to look at the carnage, searing an image onto my brain that time has never healed even all these decades later. Uncle Forrest was still sat at the kitchen table, clutching a glass of milk which now sported a thick crack down the side, allowing the liquid to slowly dribble out. He had been struck in the head by this thing, which had twisted his neck rightwards at a grotesque ninety-degree angle and torn his lower jaw away from his face, leaving it dangling there attached by a single strip of sinew. The eye I could see was rotated inwards, showing only white. On the floor lay Liv, cut clean in half at the belly, her open halves spilling out onto the floor. She lay on her chest, a face of utter terror staring up at us, her long, broken nails digging into the floorboards as if she had been desperately trying to crawl across the room but hadn't actually moved. Aunt Liv was still alive, and desperately mouthing us a message with her last moments. Run, run, she said. Her bloody hand reached out for me grasping at air as I held her daughter's face in my chest. Run. Run.

I wanted to save her. I wanted to help, to do something, anything, but I didn't know how. Her mouth continued to flap up and down, mouthing that single word as we both stood there in the kitchen completely frozen in fear and grief. Finally a sound emanated from her mouth, a shrill, cold cry of desperation. Her eyes widened, filled with desperate fear, and she dropped cold and silent on the floor.

I took Sasha in my arms and we fled that place blindly into the night. We ran for the trees, entering some distance before I tripped and we both fell. On the ground I realised we were both in our nightgowns and barefoot and if we were to get away safely, we should have at least tried to grab something on the way out. I even left the lantern back there. All was quiet at the house. I crept back a little, spying on the ruinous place from a good distance. All was quiet and still. Suddenly I saw movement at the front portion of the house - the family dog, Akaya, a large black lab, emerged from the open front door and stood on the wooden porch staring right at me. She stopped in her tracks. I tried to beckon her over to us without making a sound but still, she stood there not moving.

"Akaya!" Sasha squealed, I didn't realise she'd snuck up behind me. I shushed her harshly. The dog's tail wagged. She began to move towards us.

We watched the dog hop off the porch and across the garden, turning into a shadowy shape as it came away from the moonlight into the shadow of the pines. Then the shadow parted and the front section of the dog split from the back section, and two formless shadows began twisting and crawling across the grass emanating a terrible clicking sound like a broken typewriter. They rose up to humanoid proportions, two spindly legs, a body and a head but no arms and they looked there momentarily in the shade of the trees, despicable shadows, crooked, evil, staring at two helpless children.

They came, skittering across the grass with unimaginable speed, clicking and writhing and changing shape. We ran. My god we ran for our lives. Tripping, stumbling, getting cuts and scrapes from branches in the darkness. Into the night. Into the darkness, fleeing from the crawling terror.

Sunday, November 24th, 1963.

First published by Punk Noir Magazine, June 2023.

A lone bluebottle danced about the bright hues of the ceiling lights. *God, it must stink in here,* George thought to himself. He hadn't showered, or even changed since Friday morning in Dallas. He was now back in DC, trapped in this stifling, windowless room. So much had happened since that morning's shower. So much; it was difficult to comprehend for the public, let alone those involved. Tears flooded his eyes, blurring his vision, dazzling him. He looked back down at the table's surface. The scratches. The marks. Forgotten weathered memories of confined convicts and traitors far more evil than he could ever be, but what he had done would surpass even the vilest of criminal acts.

He sucked at his cigarette, his fourth in a half-hour, forehead resting on his spare palm, watching his tears splash onto the table's scars. There was no coming back from the brink. His bleary eyes danced over the creased lapel of his serviceman's blazer, the string of fabric poking out from the left one where they'd torn off and confiscated his American flag pin-badge.

He could hear a voice, muffled, far away, not his own. *Oh yeah, I'm not alone,* he thought to himself. The lonely bubble of remorse popped. The female voice broke through. The voice of Lydia Breckenridge - government hyena. The apathetic federal psychoanalyst.

"George, we've been over this," said Breckenridge, a slight left tilt of her head, feigning concern.

"How am I ever going to live with this?! I did this. I'll be public enemy number one for the rest of my life." George did not look up from the table.

"Only if you don't listen! George, it's all taken care of. We have our solution. I can tell you now, with some relief, that Oswald is dead."

"Dead!? Already?? How?" George dropped his hands to the table, looking across to Lydia with shock and fear. If they managed to dispose of Oswald in a single weekend, how much time would *he* have?

"Jack Ruby shot him in the chest this morning in the basement parking lot of the Dallas headquarters. He died this afternoon. Kept his mouth shut until the end."

"Holy shit... How on earth did they let that happen? And who the fuck is Jack Ruby?"

"Some club owner in town," said Breckenridge, glancing down at her myriad of notes. "A local eccentric linked to the Chicago Outfit and the FBI. I don't think he's much more than a pimp to be honest. He thought he was being some big hero avenging the president. He was *so* taken aback when they slapped bracelets on him and carted him off. He thought they would carry him out on their shoulders, not by the armpits, poor fuck."

"You told me that Oswald called himself a patsy. What if it's proved that he was? What happens when the truth comes out?"

"The empirical truth behind his motives doesn't matter anymore. America is searching for *her* truth. They captured him, they found his little sixth-floor lookout spot at the book depository, they found the gun he used, they found the shells he discharged. He killed a cop too, that is for certain. Nobody in their right mind believes he was a patsy George, not even his wife. Did you know he renounced his American citizenship? He wanted more than anything to be a commie spy for Russia. He went to live there for three years, to chase the communist dream. Turns out when you don't have any valuable information for the KGB and aren't anything more than a cry-baby wife-beating weirdo narcissist, Mother Russia ain't all it's cracked up to be. Came back with his tail between his legs didn't he. Wanted to make a name for himself. A name the phoney western communist party would remember forever. It doesn't happen like that. Life is not a dream. You and I both know this. Oswald's voice is gone, Ruby will rot for depriving America of justice. You should consider this a blessing. See it for what it is; an opportunity."

"An opportunity?! That's sick! That's missing the whole point! with Oswald dead, that leaves me as the open target. They've got to blame somebody, you said it yourself, nobody will see his assassination today as justice. They'll want someone living to blame. Someone to parade in the streets. They'd lynch him right there in on Elm Street at the exact spot it all happened if they had the chance. The whole country must be hungry for blood right now."

"You're not thinking clearly George."

"Not thinking clearly?! *Not thinking clearly?!* How the fuck would you feel if you'd just done what I did!? Would you be able to think straight? I'm gonna spend the rest of my life in jail, however short that life will be when the word gets out, and you're sitting there calm as a cucumber, talking like nothing has happened!"

A quiet pause filled the room. Breckenridge needed to play this carefully. A lot is riding on this man playing the game. *Jesus Hickey, get your shit together,* she thought. Presently, she continued confronting the broken man.

"It's no secret, everyone wanted the president dead, George. There are too many fingers being pointed in too many directions to notice you were even in the plaza on Friday. LBJ insisted that he be sworn in as the new president on board air force one, two hours after

Kennedy died. *Two hours.* Kennedy's body was on that plane. Jackie was on that plane, standing right next to Johnson! Did you see the photo?" George shook his head. "She didn't even change out of her bloody clothes! 'Let them see what they did to him', she said. It's a circus. The mob wanted him dead. Hoover wanted him dead. The CIA wanted him dead. Not to mention the communists. Shit, he had his fingers in so many wives I'm surprised they don't say that Oswald was a jealous cuck obsessed with Marilyn Monroe or something. People have been saying Kennedy is responsible for her death for months."

Another long silence filled the room. George was trying to put the pieces of the puzzle together in his head, but there were just too many to process.

"I can't live with this," he sobbed.

"You will. You have to. The country is counting on it."

"There were so many witnesses."

"The only witnesses we have, were in that car with you. They are all being debriefed as well."

"So what then? You send me off to go and rot in a room like this with my mouth shut and everything carries on like justice was served against Oswald?"

"No, you are going to keep talking with me until I am positive that we have straightened all of this out for you. Yes, the buck stops at Oswald. You and your colleagues are all currently on leave for stress until you are strong enough to accept that Oswald killed Kennedy, not you. Once you are ready and able, you will return to your origional position as a member of the secret service under our new president, Lyndon B. Johnson."

"Get the fuck out of here. That's madness!"

"It has been ordered by Johnson himself."

"...But I killed the man I swore to protect with my own life."

"Oswald killed Kennedy, George. You are under Johnson's protection. You may have vicariously done him a massive favour."

"How does any of this make sense? I should be locked away forever! Sent to the chair!"

"That is exactly how conspiracy breeds. If nobody suspects you now, how will it look if you're sent to the penitentiary? Everything would fall into chaos, even if we sentence you with some bogus, trumped-up charge. We already have our scapegoat, and as of this afternoon, he can no longer speak for himself. You will return to your previous position and the matter will be left where it lies. Right here, in this room."

"How did nobody else see what I did?!"

"Because Oswald was shooting at Kennedy. We're almost certain he did shoot him. John Conally took one of those bullets. Nobody was looking at you, they were watching the president get shot. They were trying to locate the shooter. There is no evidence of what you did. No photographs, no footage. It is a miracle."

"So I have to live with this secret all my life?"

"Only if you want your country to remain whole George."

Breckenridge sighed. Leaning back in her chair, she eyed the man who had killed the president. The man who blew Kennedy's brains all over his own wife. There had to be a way to get through to this poor sap. *The answer will come,* she thought.

"I'm going to step out for a minute George," she said, standing to attention. "Would you like some coffee? Something to eat? It's getting late, you must be hungry."

"No, thank you," said George.

Breckenridge left the room and crossed the hallway. She leant back against the cool wall for a second or two to gather her thoughts. It didn't take her long to intuit she wasn't alone.

"He's a weak one," she said, still staring at the opposing wall, the door of George's cell.

"Yes. It is going to take some tact." A male voice, gravelly with age, whisky and cigars echoed down the hall. Lydia turned to face the stranger. A tall, pale figure in an unmarked black suit stood a good few feet away. Lydia rightened herself and stepped to the man.

"What do you suppose we do, sir?" she asked.

"You may have him for the rest of today, doctor," said the man. "Tomorrow he is being sent to Aberdeen."

"Aberdeen? ...Proving Grounds?"

"Precisely."

"You're sending him to Edgewood aren't you."

"There are issues with this situation, Doctor Breckenridge, that we cannot afford to have slip through our fingers. I assume that you are familiar, in name at least, with Operation MKUltra?"

"Yes. I am vaguely familiar with the program, though not academically."

"There is a man in Edgewood right now, who is the best neurologist in the country. He runs a programme there, specialising in a phenomena called Retrograde Amnesia. Familiar?"

Breckenridge nodded, understanding what this meant for the poor man inside that room.

"Our little problem will be entered into the program tomorrow, and all of those little issues he is struggling with will be removed by Christmas."

"Isn't that a little too soon? I've only just begun speaking with him."

"The man has said enough. He has shown his hand for all of us to see. Too much remorse, Miss Breckenridge. He's going to burst eventually. We need to break the rabid dog and put him back where he belongs at our heels."

"Is there really no other option?" Lydia asked the man.

"You have tried logic and reason. The man is too far gone with what he did. If we lock him away, it'll only raise questions. He'll just tell someone from prison. Same thing as if we dispose of him. His absence will garner questions. They're asking questions about everyone who was there already. He needs to be placed under control for all of this to play out how Johnson wants it to."

"Okay, I understand." Said Breckenridge with subservience.

The two of them walked down the remainder of the corridor, away from George Hickey's cell, and entered the lobby, both heading for the building's security clearance, headed for the exit.

"Aren't you going back to speak to him?" Asked the man.

"No, I'm going home," said Breckenridge. "He's done for."

George Hickey jr, among several other secret servicemen, was heavily hungover the morning of Friday November 22nd, 1963. Situated in the car driving directly behind the president, Hickey targeted the location of Lee Harvey Oswald after his first shot hit the road. Hickey, with his eyes on the Book Depository, reached for the AR-15 tucked under his seat, a gun he was unfamiliar with. The safety was released on the AR-15 - Oswald fired his second shot, hitting Kennedy and Connally. The two cars suddenly sped up amidst the panic. Hickey lost his balance, fell back and pulled the trigger of the rifle, which at that moment was aimed squarely at the back of Kennedy's head.

The rest, as they say, is history.

Call Me Grishka

Down And Out In 'Dam

A frigid air crawled down from the Northeast, crossing the Markermeer and settling down in the damp cobbles of the city. A riverworn pontoon boat was coming with the breeze, and its single passenger was a stranger to the country. The vessel chugged quietly through the night air, sending ripples of chilled water about, disturbing the buoys' sleep. The lonesome boat made its heading, resting snug up against the jetty, and the stranger alighted the boat before it could come to a complete stop, crossing the palm of the helmsman with some weighty reward mid-stride and he slunk off into the night without a word. The helmsman, a local fisherman named Ned, waited a few seconds before he released his stomach into the black water of the river - once the coast was clear of his guest of course. He watched his stomach's contents dissipate into the dark waters wondering what on earth he had experienced. What an awful hot stench the man had carried about him! He was the most peculiar fellow Ned had ever seen and was twice charismatic as he was foul in presentation. His husband, upon his eventual return home that night, would complain about the weight of the stink he brought in with him, infesting his clothes over the usual stench of fish, but nevertheless, his complaints did take a back seat when he realised the weight of his husband's paycheck. It turned out that Ned had been given upwards of a thousand euros for his twelve euro lift along with his agreed discretion. This did not, however, shoo a sincere interrogation.

"Well, who do you think it was?" Asked his husband inquisitively.

"Some creepy, rich tourist with more money than sense," He replied, and this is how it was left for both of them, at Ned's insistence, for if his intuitive mind had won hence, there would be no believing in the truth of reality. He'd jump into the water, the justified death of a true madman. There was no way that the man was who Ned thought he was when he first laid eyes on him. Absolutely no way.

The black-clad wanderer moved stealthily with the shadows, as was his wont, in that dreary midnight Amsterdam. As beautiful as the city night was, serenity has no bearing on the doing of business, especially business which requires the sneaking of its participants. Treading as lightly as he could upon the cobbles he was, his hard-soled cordovan boots echoing across empty windows and over the quiet streets with each step when suddenly a ruckus blew out from inside a quiet tavern ahead, with five musclebound oafs spilling into the street before him, laughing and bantering at each other's inebriated expense.

"Tourists," the stranger thought to himself, "and what is worse, British tourists. Grishka despises British tourists."

Like a bat disturbed from some deep slumber he flew across the street and up the nearest alleyway away from the louts, up towards the lights that shine red in the night, and there, like a fly caught in a web, he was trapped. Three street vultures were already set upon pecking at him before he had the opportunity to flee, and in their presence he felt completely disgusted. The tallest of the three, a cherry-haired beauty clad in ruby red lingerie, thigh high leather boots and an oversized black fur coat, addressed him directly.

"Wat dacht je van een dans?" She asked.

"Grishka does not require dance," the stranger replied. "Fill your belly with other man's snail grease tonight, wild mongrel."

"Come on baby," the prostitute responded, now in English, "we show you a good time for a good price."

"You not know good time if it smacks you in face," said Grishka, aggressively pushing past the three women and setting off down the street.

The air about them all had begun to change. This was not an ordinary meeting of night owls in the midnight chill, and something had piqued Grishka's senses as he was fleeing from the night ladies. His hair stood on end. His lengthy, bedraggled beard twitched. His undercarriage tingled. Something foul was happening in the street behind him.

"Stay your claws creatures," he roared, turning his head ninety degrees, a small, single horn visibly penetrating through his greasy fringe. "Now is not time to tarry with the likes of you."

The three women were moving up close behind him, and their demeanour had changed. They all seemed taller and their eyes gave off a furious scarlet gleam reflecting from the lights of the red dancing windows.

"But we wish to treat with the great Grishka this night!" Squealed the shorter, plump woman. "Don't go! We won't let you go! It is once in a lifetime you get to set your eyes on such renown!"

The three women rose up, nightmarish and hostile, demonic faces of succubi evil, their breasts spilling from their tight clothing as they grew in size before him, upwards of nine feet tall. Sinewy wings spread about them and they began to flap and squeal in a shrieking frenzy. Grishka sighed. There was no escape. No peace, no rest from the ills of the world. Slowly he turned about, facing the three harpies hovering above him.

"Listen, sletten, roll up hanging titties. Enchant lesser men tonight."

But the succubi would not listen. In a shrill frenzy of squeals, claws, breasts and wings, they snatched the stranger and took him up high above the city, tearing at his flesh, biting him, clawing him with grotesque talons, long-nailed fingers grabbing at his crotch. He floundered but could not get away. The ghouls, suddenly disappointed at their prize, had a change of heart and dropped him from a great height into the river below.

"There's nothing there!" One of the beasts screamed. "Nothing at all!"

Grishka was troubled. He was losing a lot of blood and his lungs were filling with icy cold water. He sank for a bit - no sense letting the bitches know that he's still alive. When he surmised that the coast was clear, he hauled his bedraggled frame up onto the nearest jetty, his giant beard, his trench coat, his ill-fitting undershirt all serving to resemble a large soggy cat. Laying on his back upon the soaking wood of the walkway, he gazed up at the stars wondering to himself why it had all come to this. Presently, the night sky blackened - some new shape was looming over him.

"I don't understand why you must continue to draw such clamorous attention to yourself sir," a melodious voice rang out in the dark.

"Grishka did not seek harpy this night," Said Grishka. "Harpy sniff out Grishka."

"Well, come along then squire, let's get you up and out of this cold," said the voice. "The ladies won't be back I'm guessing, it looks as though you were a frightful disappointment to them!"

"Succubus could not find cock. Look in wrong place."

"Well, all is well then! That was a narrow scrape!"

"For them," Grishka scowled.

"Yes indeed" said the man emerging from the dark. He was a tall and slight gentleman with spindly arms and legs. He was dressed head to toe in baby-poo coloured tweed. A shimmering silk cravat squirmed about the open collar of his white shirt. He was Tarquin

Carmichael III, baron of Medinia and consort to his mighty Grishka, whom he loved above all others.

Despite the malicious attack, Grishka showed no wounds, a phenomenon that hadn't phased Tarquin. This was far from the first time. He leaned down and picked up his master by the armpits, setting him onto his feet, and brushed the algae from his soaking trench coat.

"Why my lord, it appears as though you are missing a boot!" Tarquin exclaimed.

"Yes," replied Grishka. "It is somewhere in the harbour. Grishka will not make you fetch it."

"A verily kind master you are my lord." Said Tarquin. "Do you still have it?"

Grishka checked his coat. "Yes."

The two men took off into the night, Grishka leaving a trail of water and harbour slime behind them. They walked and chatted a while in the nighttime air. Grishka showed no signs of chill, and Tarquin was secretly grateful to the succubi, for giving his master a much-needed bath. Grishka refused to bathe, and while he would do anything for the one he loved, Tarquin never could grow an affection for his master's musk. They were headed back towards the red-light district, to the room that Tarquin had procured for them earlier in the week. It was a small one-bedroom apartment above a closed down brothel that hadn't survived the pandemic; more than enough for the two of them, for sleeping rough across Europe had become commonplace and the two of them found more comfort together on the floor than in more appropriate lodgings. There was no sign of the lady demons. They must've found fresh prey tonight. Probably a few of the brutish English bulldogs. Tarquin was relieved, Grishka wasn't phased either way.

The Noseless Ghost

Grishka dropped his wet clothes onto the wooden floorboards for Tarquin to pick up. The floor was warm, heated by hot water pipes laid underneath. Tarquin couldn't help himself. He glanced up at Grishka to get a good look. Six foot four inches tall, sinewy and strong he was, a homeless statue of David in his devout servant's eyes. Tarquin felt himself becoming aroused. Grishkas' beard twitched, his eyes flared.

"Not now Tarquin, my love." He said without looking. "There will be time later."

Grishka was holding up a curious object, which he had pulled from his wet coat. It looked like the skull of a small creature, though what creature exactly, remained a mystery. He packed the eye socket of the thing with a thick, black substance like clay and washed it with the flame of a chrome zippo. He pursed his lips to the creature's horn and sucked a lungful of smoke out of it, blowing a ream of smoke into Tarquin's face. Tarquin couldn't handle opiates and Grishka knew it. The residual smoke knocked the man over onto his back and he lay there, numb and lifeless without protest. Grishka laid down on his back, skull in hand, rhythmically taking drags of the sticky black tar, drifting off on the ether, riding the waves to god knows where. He lifted the laminated photograph he had also rescued from his clothing and stared at it wistfully. It was worn; a black and white portrait of a very regal-looking woman.

"Oh Alex," he wailed. "Grishka misses you. We may see each other again one day."

"Oh give it a break, Grishka, son of Yefim!" An invisible voice responded. "A century is long enough to pine over the bullet-ridden corpse of the Tsarina!"

"And for over a hundred years you have haunted my steps Guseva, you noseless pig! Get away, Grishka is enjoying quiet time with his Alex!"

Guseva, a grotesque and frightening looking woman with a missing nose, appeared translucent above Grishka. Tarquin could not see her, but he knew too well of her presence. He rolled over foetal and went to sleep on the floor, ignoring his master and the ghost. Guseva drifted around the room, her manly frame warping in the fog of her being.

"I come with news, Griska," she said.

"More lies. Lies and nothing more from the noseless ghost." Grishka sneered.

"No, no lies this time. We all know what it is you are looking for."

"If you are going to tell me that you know where that is, Grishka will eat his belt before believing in ripe donkey shit."

"I will admit, it is but a rumour Grish," said the ghost "But I have reason to believe that what you are looking for is in the United Kingdom."

"Urgh! English pigs! You are doing this on purpose, Gusava the mollusk. You would have Grishka crawl around in the last place on earth he would want to be just for the fun of following him!"

"If that was the case, I would have told you to look for it in America."

Grishka dry-heaved at the sheer thought of it. How grotesque. How unlike the motherland the kingdom of narcissism was. He shivered. There was no richer hell to him.

"Guseva has led Grishka astray many times before," Said Grishka. "What is different? What brings Grishka to being foolish enough to trip the ghost-pig's trap?"

"This is true, and I don't expect you to trust me this time, but I am tired, Grish. I am tired of having to follow you around, to plague you. I want to rest. It's been a long century. Maybe if you actually find it you will find some closure. I could be free."

"Free?" Grishka sneered. "What makes you think Grishka wants Gusava to be free? All these long years we have wandered! What a wasteful end to a charming time eh!"

"An end is all it needs to be," Said Gusava. "You will do what you want, as you have always done. If you decide to go and look there, you know where to find me."

With that, the ghost disappeared. Grishka lay back, clutching the old photo. Could it really be true? Was it in England of all places? Tarquin stirred on the floor. He mumbled some incoherent words and fell still again. Grishka wondered if he should rouse his companion with his mouth - some meditation through a serious power-bottoming session could do them both good, but he decided against it for the moment. He had thoughts to process. Was the lying ghost being truthful? He had no reason to believe that she was and he was in no mood for another fruitless goose-chase. This would need some serious consideration and more to the point, he needed to replace his boot.

The Vampir Of Amsterdam

A few hours later, Tarquin was awoken by something soft and girthy entering his mouth. He knew what to do instinctively, for it wasn't the first time he had consumed his master's 'cock demons'. He lathered the thing up with his tongue and a half a pint of salty fluid slithered down his throat. Grishka took the foot-long object and tucked it into his coat.

"We go," he said. "After you fetch boot."

It was late afternoon when Tarquin returned with a boot he had swiped from a store in town with some minor misdirection. It was a different colour to the one his master owned, but that did not matter.

He brought food for himself which he ate at a small table whilst Grishka paced the room, twitching uncontrollably, his piercing eyes changing hue.

"I do not want to go there," he huffed out loud to himself.

"Well I hate to be the bearer of bad news sire, but you may have no other choice. We don't have any other leads other than the one which led us here. I suggest we follow up with this situation first, then figure out what to do when the time is right."

"Well then, how do you suggest we find him?" Said Grishka.

"I have a feeling we won't need to sir. Iliodor will probably already know about your presence in the city by now, if there are harpies here, there are vampires, and news between them spreads quickly."

"Very well. We squeeze the whores tonight."

The couple waited until the night was at its apex before they returned to the red-light district. They found the same three women as before in the same place, but now they were joined by a dark and imposing figure.

"Well, well well," said the figure, turning his gaze to the approaching duo. "If it isn't the mad monk himself. Nice to see you, old friend."

"Iliodor. It pains Grishka to see you living," said Grishka.

"Living? No. I am not alive. I have not been alive since 1952. But you already knew that didn't you Rasput..."

"Do not speak that name to Grishka!" Snapped Grishka.

"You called me Iliodor. Nobody has called me that in three parts of a century."

"Fine. Sergei. Your time has come. You pay for your crimes against God. We have come far to find you."

"Poor, poor Grishka. How old are you now? A hundred and fifty? Yet still the same naive and cockless fool you ever were. You will die here finally tonight, putrid Khlysty!"

Grishka ordered Tarquin away and he fled, pushing through the crowd of tourists who had begun to gather in the street, gawking at the ruckus. Rasputin turned to the group, his magical eyes taking them immediately.

"So you come to see the show eh?" He winked. Each of the dozen men and women climaxed, right then and there. One particularly excited American pulled open the back door to the adjacent nightclub and booming drum and bass began to flood the street. The stage was set.

Grishka drew his weapons. In one hand he held his severed foot-long penis which was glowing with a purple light at the tip and in the other hand, a large golden crucifix. The harpies had changed once more into their monstrous forms and stripped their clothing completely. Some of the crowd fled in fear, others were transfixed. Most of them were still aroused. The creatures set upon Grishka in a frenzy, but this time he was having none of it. The claws of the first came, swiping at his face. These he dodged, crooking his back unnaturally to the left at 90 degrees. He began to sing, a deep basso profundo drone roaring from deep in his throat in tune to the nightclub music. As the first harpy flew by him, the second came down from above, face first. Grishka blasted her in the face with the crucifix, causing her to flip upwards in pain. Once the demon was right way up, up came the holy dong, entering her between the legs. The Harpy's belly swelled with a bright purple light and she released a scream that was heard in Bruges.

"Idi na hui!" Grishka screamed, and the harpy exploded in a deluge of gore. The remaining two harpies waivered. The first one came for another swipe, this time from the rear, and Grish dropped to the lotus prayer position, causing her to miss once again and fly over his head. He grabbed a foot and slammed her to the ground, leaping up and pinning her down, the crucifix between his knee and her chest. He beat her about the face with the truncheon-cock.

"Chtob tebe deti v'sup srali!" He yelled, and the harpy disintegrated into a cloud of bloody vapour.

The third harpy, who had not moved from her place beside Iliodor, spread her wings in attack position, leaped into the air and up into the night sky. She was never seen in Europe again. Iliodor cursed the creature under his breath. He stepped forward, meeting with Grishka a few paces apart. Grishka gripped his club. He held up the crucifix and Iliodor winced at the sight of it. The vampire reached into the pocket of his black suit and pulled out a silver-coloured object. Out and out of his pocket it came, until he held in his hands a nine-foot spear. Grishka quaked in his mismatched boots for the first time in many, many years.

"Where… where did Sergei get that?!" He wailed.

"I took it from the cold dead hands of Saint Hitler himself, Grishka." Said Iliodor with dreadful authority. "This is it. The Lance of Longinus. You didn't think I'd face you empty handed did you?"

Grishka felt a deep existential dread crawl through his bowels. The spear that pierced Christ's side on the cross. This fiend had it all along. What terror. What a precious and dangerous relic. He could see the white flames flicker within the cold metal head of the spear. He was already defeated in his mind.

Synesthetic Therapy: Decadent Meditation For The Middle Class Eccentric.

Session 1: The Woe Mule.

Can you hear that smell? That! There, over yonder. Betwixt the Cafe Nero and the council flats. Yes. The alleyway between glory and wretchedness where Francis Bellamy used to piss. It's almost like it was when you were a bairn, but not really. It's all grey now. We can all hear it you know, laying all on us like a wet blanket. It smells like pledge and almonds. The smooth springtime breeze of the collective unconscious, collectively reminding you all that you are an individual, just like everybody else. Now, come out the other end, lay back sea-level on your most downy cushion and take a single deep breath. Fill your wet chest bags with air, and let that air slowly leak out like an old balloon. Now seal the lower ocular skin flaps to the upper ocular skin flaps, covering your globular optic light receptors. Just the ones on your face please, for the time being at least. Keep those face cameras closed up nice and tight like the door seal of a brand-new washing machine. You will now find yourself inside of yourself. You're welcome and welcome home, please wipe your feet on the mat provided and be sure that the draught excluder is firmly set in place.

ADDENDUM: If you have followed the steps provided verbatim thus far, it is important to note it may be of use to read the full instructions before acting upon them, as closing your face windows will result in your inability to read further on. If you had already realised the conundrum and instead chose to read on, congratulations you delightful little lollipop, and if you have yet to, then take your time sitting there in your head-bucket all alone until epiphany decides to rescue you, or death takes you. Or... Failing that, something in between... Like a toilet emergency.

Now you are relaxed. All of those eyes closed, drifting off in a kayak on the tide of your own subconsciousness, trying your hardest to not think about the dark times. The debt. The anxiety. Crippling depression. Illness or death of a loved one. Perhaps some bad touches in your past that you've tried to lock away inside of some kind of egg. Maybe you shouldn't think about the time you blamed that mess you made on the cat - when you got carried away in self love with the rubber ducky and tripped over, breaking that special vase and impulse made you blame the carnage on the Dinko, who was subsequently kicked outside in the rain and was squashed by a rover. The car, not the dog. Do not think of these things. Do not think of that embarrassing moment that nibbles away at your head when you try to sleep at night. When everybody looked at you in disapproval and your cheeks boiled up hot as beef. that one moment which is always rapping away at your headbox like a coked-up woodpecker. No. We let the Woe Mule carry the load. He's right there. Over there by the shore. He cannot swim in your memories or he'd drown, you selfish ninny, you'll have to row your canoe down there yourself and ask him what he wants in return.

Sometimes it's coffee, sometimes it's a cake of uranium 235. Sometimes he wants tickets to see Billie Eilish and we all know how hard they are to get hold of. They sell out in minutes. They're bought wholesale by scalpers. Something must be done about this injustice.

Anyway, it all depends on the weight and circumference of your woes. The Woe Mule understands the value of carrying such a thick load for you and will not be bartered with.

We have now reached the shore. We have jumped spryly out of the boat and felt the soft comforting shards of mind shingle poking our toes. It is time to approach the Woe Mule. Now it must be said, as an important note too I may add, that just as regular old earthly farm mules, you must not approach the Woe Mule from behind, lest you receive a sharp kick to the loins, and as the Woe Mule transcends time, space and consciousness, you will feel the impact of hoof on soft bits in your waking plane. Approach and courtesy to the fantastical mule and he will weigh your pain and offer his price. What will it be? A well shorn topiary? An army of bees? Or a specific limb from an unspecific ocelot?

This and more about your inner self shall indeed be discovered - in Session 2: Cotton Candy Oneness.

Three, two, one...

Awaken, feeling refreshed and relaxed having begun your journey with us. Now please return all trays to the upright position and place all borrowed pencils back into the jars provided. Don't forget to bring your own baggage with you next week if you forgot to today. Good will, good luck and good riddance.

Session 2: Cotton Candy Oneness.

A pastel blue alien boy named Milton once told me that he wants to fill me with eggs. I am not yet at full capacity. What secrets would YOU like to share today? Perhaps we should just resume where we left off from last week's session, lest we dig a guilt hole with a blackmail shovel.

You will know by now, the prize wished for by the wonderful Woe Mule is indeed a thermos flask filled with Olive's oil and eyebrow shame. It is important at this juncture to mention that you shouldn't ask the purpose of his prize, for the Woe Mule is a cosmic behemoth wandering the shores of the river of subconscious and you could not possibly fathom what use he may have for any item he may choose. Besides, he's ruddy sick of hearing it. You are lucky though, for the infinite plain of the subconscious is both unending and fallible, and so you can just conjure up what he wants with your head and give him all your troubles for him to carry with ease. But do not let your plastic guard down or take your mask off, for the Woe Mule will continue to follow you, carrying your woes, wherever you go. They haven't permanently gone for cigarettes like your dad did when you were twelve.

Let us venture a level deeper. Open the mahogany hatch. Climb down the ladder. Turn on the light bulbs with some flirtatious words and off we go. What delights are there? I don't know. I haven't written those words yet.

You are now good and deep in the stomach of your mind, descending deeper and deeper into the acid wash dungarees of your thoughts and feelings. Don't venture too deep though, not just yet. The deeper within your soul you go, the more irreversible damage you can cause (see scientology for more details). The butterfly effect works on space as well as time unfortunately, so it is important that you stay within the car at all times and keep your hands down lest they become spaghettified.

You get to the end of the hallway. There's a door. Open it up. You have the key. Look down. Yes, on the lanyard. The green one, not the mauve. Pop open that door now and go inside. What can you see? Darkness? Turn on the light. It's OK, it's an energy saver, just give it a moment to warm up. Now, what do you see? No, that's not it. That's not it either. That's a tin of lumpfish caviar. Over there. Down there in the far-left corner. The duffle. Yes! Now let us part the flaps and discover the insides. Liberate the shiny golden pegs from their hooped oppressors. Let's take a peek. What's in there? Is it legs? Is it porcelain? Is it batman bubble bath? No. It is cotton candy oneness.

Taste it. Taste the cotton candy oneness. Press your tongue on it. What does it mean? Is it happy, or is it grapefruit flavour? Be careful not to salivate too much, for wet makes the cotton candy clump, and you'll have a lump of pure uncut concentrated oneness slip down your neck like a nice wad of caramelly phlegm. Doesn't it feel ripe?

The warm in your belly like a bowl of tomato soup juice. Pure sweetened oneness. The true quality in the healing power of omnipotent sugar in strand form.

Three... two... one... we are now back in your shameful bedsit.

Session 3: Stalkerness, Rattles And Jangles.

Good Tuesday. Now is not the time to be recalcitrant. Please resume the position, close those kneecaps and go up into the pleasurable inky black. Nice and cold like a delicious wet blanket on your face. Now suck in some air. Not too hard, not like a Dyson, you might not make it back. More like your mum's old hoover from 1982 that she still insists is perfectly fine although it won't even pick up dandruff off a hardwood floor. I know it may feel like cosmic waterboarding at first, but I promise we'll be back to where we were in no time.

If you have followed the steps correctly thus far, you should have given all of your worry sacks over to the Woe Mule to carry and filled your belly all big and plump with cotton candy oneness. If this is not the case, you may have to pay again for the first two sessions. In fact I implore you to, I'd like a new espresso machine.

We are now amongst the trees and ashes. Try not to squish any of the bugs with your heels, they are Jehovahs witnesses and will just make you feel bad. I must also stress kindly that you avoid any rattles or jangles, Mr Gethard lives in the forest and he smells your colours. Best to avoid him sniffing you or your noises. You know he likes your shape. You've hidden him away deep in here for a reason, best keep it that way for now.

Follow the well trodden path and stick to it. If you leave the path, you will find yourself navel high in sick and mudge. Follow the oaks until they become horse-chestnuts and join a colourful sprite in a game of conkers. Which colour sprite will you invite? Pink, purple or blue?

Can't change your mind now.

Pink, like pigskin, is the sprite of undying fantasy. She will spin you a yarn in exchange for... Well, yarn. Be warned though, she believes fervently in the flat earth and will chew at your tendons if you try to refute her claims.

Purple, like the bruise on your face, is the sprite of lost objects. Ask her where any item lost past or present is, and she will gladly oblige, in exchange for saliva or hairs.

Blue, like your current mood, is the sprite of chains and is into some terribly kinky stuff. Be prepared for some incredibly kinky stuff. I know that's what you wanted, or you wouldn't have chosen blue, you cheeky gecko.

Oh, good lord spirit of the great beyond, your battle of conkers has created much rattles and several jangles. Here comes old Mr Gethard!! He has discovered your shape and wants to know your current address! Please now spin those legs and get into a little run! What will happen now?! You're right near to those things you trapped down far away! Those snotty horrid little things you buried deep down in your cabbage patch. Don't let them swarm in you like bees! I feel it best to eject for now and perhaps we shall resume next week properly prepared and armed with sticks and snakes.

Session 4: The Depth Of A Navel.

Let's dive straight back into it. Diving in deep and fast like tearing a scab on accident. You are now caught up inside by Mr Gethard. We did warn you to keep the quips and japes to yourself. Oh woe. Stuck like old untouched elderflower cordial in a sun-stained bottle. A veritable oubliette of misery, but don't fret, he has yet to unzip his body bag, let alone cover you in salty webs. Don't let your eye bags fill with worrisome pitty drops though, this is not the end. This is liminal space. Sometimes to transition from crystal meth to crystal glasses, you've got to suffer through a few public Burger King toilet freakouts. The shame will haunt you for the rest of your life and mould your grey clay into that of a better being. Defecating naked on the floor aside, if you do find yourself in a situation where the choice is Burger King or a Waterstones, you're better off eating books.

Mr Gethard's principal weakness is the depth of his navel. He keeps all his secrets in there. Keys, nautical charts. An abacus. Ironically no space for fluff. If you check the watch pocket of your levi's you'll find a conch of considerable density, you can use to ram the nook. He will yelp in pain and recoil in defence of his belly secrets. Now flee!! Like a gazelle born in pure unadulterated freedom!!! Follow the light! You are free of woe! Free of nonces! Free of jelly!

Three... we're coming back.

Two... back to reality

One... back to your lonely terrible little pustule of a life.

You are awake, conscious and clear. My work here is done. If you have suffered an accident on therapy that was not your fault, kindly call cosmic claims direct, my side hustle, and I'll be sure to milk your little teats for everything else you've got. One love, dear squeeze.

About the author

Bam Barrow is an East Anglian based writer of occult fiction and folk horror with an unquenchable thirst for the dark, mysterious and extreme tenants of human behaviour. He has had works published in Grinning Skull Press & Punk Noir Magazine. Look out for his collection of short stories 'The CVLT of CTHXS', releasing with Translucent Eyes Press next year.

Also available from Urban Pigs Press

A hard-hitting collection of equally gritty and compelling stories. Jenkins has harvested his finest pieces from across his journey into the darkest reaches of his imagination. True brit grit delivered on an indigestible platter combining filthy realism with tones of dark humour. From twisted gangland gratuitous violence to the litter addled riverbanks, Jenkins probes at our worst fears and exposes the pitfalls of toxic masculinity.

"Simple Britishness and quintessentially approved ideology slowly tears itself apart in this fast paced and gripping collection, exposing the British Isles and all its darlings across a glass written, and played, so very darkly."

– Joseph Runnacles

URBAN PIGS PRESS

https://urbanpigspress.co.uk/

Printed in Great Britain
by Amazon

37284047R00099